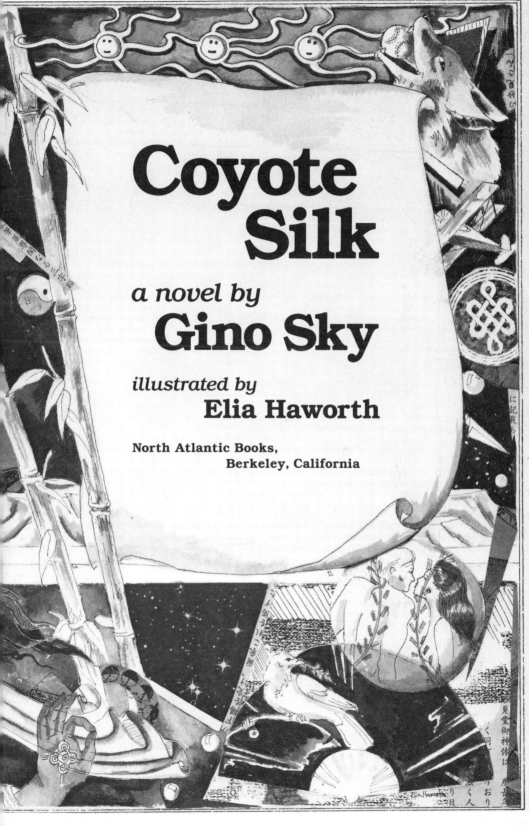

Coyote Silk

a novel by
Gino Sky

illustrated by
Elia Haworth

North Atlantic Books,
Berkeley, California

Other Titles by Gino Sky

Novel   *Appaloosa Rising*
             The Legend of The Cowboy Buddha

Poetry   *Sweet Ass'd Angels*
             Jonquil Rose
             The Ball Tournament Specialist
             The Great Medicine Trail

Coyote Silk

Copyright © 1987 by Gino Sky

ISBN 0-938190-92-X (paperback)
ISBN 0-938190-93-8 (cloth)

Published by North Atlantic Books
          2320 Blake Street
          Berkeley, California 94704

Cover art and illustrations by Elia Haworth
Cover and book design by Paula Morrison
Typeset by Classic Typography

This project is partially supported by a grant from the National Endowment for the Arts, a federal agency.

Coyote Silk is sponsored by the Society for the Study of Native Arts and Sciences, a nonprofit educational corporation whose goals are to develop an ecological and crosscultural perspective linking various scientific, social, and artistic fields; to nurture a holistic view of arts, sciences, humanities, and healing; and to publish and distribute literature on the relationship of mind, body, and nature.

Library of Congress Cataloging-in-Publication Data

Sky, Gino.
    Coyote silk / Gino Sky.
       p.   cm.
     ISBN 0–938190–93–8 : $20.00   ISBN 0–938190–92–X (pbk.) : $9.95
     I. Title.
    PS3569.K9C6 1987
    813'.54—dc19   87–22387
                                             CIP

The author wishes to give special thanks to Nancy Sullivan for The Cowboy Buddha Hotel, Diann Grimm for Holding Friendship, Brenda Nelson for Keeping Faith, Muddi Wallace for Flying Clouds, Elia Haworth for Intimissimo, Rosalie Sorrels for Dancing With Bears, Nancy Stringfellow for Dancing with Walter, Richard Grossinger for Following Through. This book was written in the spirit of my ancestors and dedicated to my two daughters, Nichole Bhatti-Sky and Shoni Sky.

For Hosteen Klah — The Buddha Shooting Way

Cast of Characters

Seventh Mesa

These people are called The Holy Highs or The Hall of Famers (living at the Seventh Mesa's Hall of Fame) from having reached the highest consciousness among the four mesas.

Buddha Shooting Way

Jesus

Holy Man

Holy Woman

Pollen Boy

Four Winds

The Mother Goddess

Confucius

Lao-tsu

Martin Luther King

Martin Luther King's Dream Speech

Mahatma Gandhi

The Cowboy Buddha

Fifth Mesa

The Holy Misfits. They are known as The Holy People and they live in a matriarchal society based on world peace and baseball.

The Great Mother

Kid Monday

Tuesday Coyote

Spider Woman

The Whoa Man

Leonardo da Vinci

April Fools

Joe Bamboo

One Hand Clapping

Thermos

Nuclear Spud

Rodeo Tai Chi

Porch Swing

Swiss Army Knife

A Rose is A Rose is A . . .

High Roller

The Flying Findhorns

Curve Ball

Air Brush

Quarterback Sneak

Cosmic Riddle

Beethoven's Fourth Piano Concerto In Something Or Other

Babe Ruth's Home Run Swing

Fourth Mesa

Living on what was once called Heaven these people are known as The Heavenites.

Mohammed	Moses
The Old Testament	Charles Darwin
Henri Matisse	

Third Mesa

Where the basic three dimensional human lives. The Third Mesa has been involved in war since the Big Bang of Creative Evolution.

Molly Rose	Ava Matisse
General May Liberty	

Children of The Third Mesa

LaMar	Sophie	Shama	Sarah
Jamal	Lisa	Scotty	Heidi
Juan	Rosie	Michi	

The Fifth Mesa's baseball stadium had been selected by The Great Mother as the site for her world peace experiment. Every seat was filled with the Holy People from 1 the Fifth Mesa, the Heavenites from the Fourth and the Seventh Mesa had sent down a prestigious group of Holy Highs from its Hall of Fame. The lights had been turned on, and the two directors of the peace project, The Great Mother and the Whoa Man, were already on the field talking with their team. If successful, all wars on the Third Mesa, which had been going on forever, would cease.

The Great Mother and The Whoa Man stepped over to the pitcher's mound as they waved to their friends. The dugouts were filled with two self-appointed cheering sections from the Fifth Mesa because they were so excited that their mesa had discovered the formula for peace. Hanging in and around the dugouts were Spider Woman, April Fools, Quarterback Sneak, Air Brush, Rodeo Tai Chi, Joe Bamboo, Thermos, and Curveball. The box seats had been reserved for their guests. From the Seventh Mesa were Buddha Shooting Way,

1

Jesus, Holy Man and Holy Woman, Pollen Boy, Four Winds. Confucius. Lao-tsu. Martin Luther King and his Dream Speech, and their lawyer and biographer, The Cowboy Buddha. From the Fourth Mesa, the Heavenites sent Moses, Mohammed, and The Old Testament.

"Come on . . . Whoa Man," came a voice from the dugout.

"Atta girl, big mama," someone shouted from the stands.

The Whoa Man, who was dressed in a tweed jacket and baggy pants, turned in a semi-circle and tipped his cowboy hat. The Great Mother reminded him that he should say something about their experiment. He took a fast look around the stadium, and then concentrated his gaze at his running shoes as he tried to think of what he wanted to say. He kicked a clod. "Well, I'm pleased that so many of you could come," he began. He scratched his kinky gray hair and made a gargoylian face. "The Great Mother should really be talking because she's the one who got me started on this project." Again, he kicked the clod. The moon was full and it looked as if it were hanging over centerfield. "So, I guess I'll just let her do the talkin'." He waved his wide brimmed hat and dumped it back onto his large head.

The Great Mother stepped up. She picked at a loose thread on the sleeve of her handmade jump suit and smiled at the audience. She had a warm face, and her eyes looked like two dark moons floating in iridescent bowls of sweet milk. Her skin was coffee in color and honey-cream in texture, and her beauty rode every movement like flute music. She waved, smiled, and held her hands. "Dear honored guests from the Fourth and Seventh Mesas," she began, as she slowly turned to look into each face, "and my beloved colleagues from the Fifth Mesa. I believe that we are on to something really big that will dramatically change the consciousness of the people on the Third Mesa." She paused to look back at the moon, and then over at The Whoa Man. "This man," she continued, as she raised one arm, "this genius of an enlightened soul appears to have perfected a way that will make what's left of the Third Mesa population stop fighting." She shook her fist and looked at the crowd. "Our lab experiments have worked out perfectly, and now we feel that we're ready to take on the consciousness of the Third Mesa."

"Who did you experiment on?" Thermos yelled from the dugout.

The Great Mother laughed. "Well, it's obvious that we couldn't use any of our own Holy People, so we used Passenger pigeons,

2

Wood bison and Tasmanian owls that my sons were able to bring back from extinction."

"Hurrah for Kid Monday's and Tuesday Coyote's genitalia vulgaris," April Fools shouted.

"Let's hear it for mental orgasms," Joe Bamboo yelled, referring to one of The Whoa Man's successful inventions.

The Great Mother's smile was a soft brushing of pink light as she thought about the experiment. She glanced at her partner. "Yes . . . we can really thank him for that."

"And Whiter-Than-White-Light," came another comment from the left field bleachers.

The Whoa Man laughed as he jammed his hands into his pockets. "Whoa. . . ," he mumbled to himself, feeling somewhat embarrassed. However, he thought to himself, even the Holy Highs had switched over to his light.

"Let's end war . . ."

"Forever . . ."

"Hallelujah brothers and sister and Amen," Moses shouted from the box seats.

"Yo . . . ," The Old Testament added, getting into the spirit of the evening.

Lao-tsu nudged Confucius. "They're the remnants from that old Western culture and they are somewhat rowdy at times, don't you think?"

Confucius nodded and rubbed his beard, "A few thousand more reincarnations perhaps and they'll come around."

"Hopefully," Lao-tsu added, "before they are promoted to the Seventh Mesa."

The Great Mother raised her hand for silence.

"What about Kid Monday?" Beethoven's Fourth Piano Concerto asked about The Great Mother's son.

The Great Mother clasped her hands and touched her lips as she thought about him. "Well, I'm happy to tell you that Kid has been in communication with us. He has been able to liberate all of the surviving Third Mesa children and they are on their way to the Fifth Mesa at this very moment."

There was a loud cheer. Several hats were thrown into the air.

"What about Tuesday?" April Fools asked about The Great Mother's youngest son, Tuesday Coyote.

She rubbed her face and shook her head. "Unfortunately,"

she answered, "we haven't been able to locate him. But, we do know that he's been involved in the war on the Third Mesa." She looked up and forced a hard smile. "But, all we can do is pray for his safety."

"This experiment will fix him right up," One Hand Clapping shouted.

"He'll come back someday," Joe Bamboo said.

"Sure he will," Nuclear Spud added. She stepped up to the pitcher's mound and gave the thumbs up.

The Great Mother nodded as she looked over at The Whoa Man. "Ready?" she asked.

"Let's do it," the scientist added.

The Great Mother clapped her hands. "Well, I guess this is it." She stepped forward. "Except to mention that this experiment was designed to permeate the entire Third Mesa with all of your auras."

"Without side effects," Nuclear Spud joked.

"Yeah," April Fools added, "we're going way beyond mental orgasms."

The Holy Highs from the Seventh Mesa's Hall of Fame looked at each other as if they couldn't believe what they had just heard. "They're going to use our auras?" Jesus asked his friends.

"That's right, baby," April Fools said, as he leaned against their box. "Since you're so busy being holier-than-thou on your country club mesa, we thought we'd at least ship down your auras so they could be working for peace." He laughed, and tapped his forehead. "Procuratus aureolus, if you dig my message."

"Hey, bug off," The Cowboy Buddha, the Holy Highs' agent yelled, "you're not using anything without a contract."

The Great Mother hurried to their box. "It's all right," she said, as she gave The Cowboy Buddha her most charming and seductive smile. We only need their presence, their serene, peaceful spirits." She looked at them and touched their hands. "You've been our teachers for so long I just want you to know how honored we are to have you here." She grabbed April Fools' ear and took him back to the dugout. "Lighten up," she whispered, "we know they haven't contributed very much for Third Mesa peace, but that's the way fame goes." She rubbed his hair and kissed his forehead. "Just remember, kiddo, they're way at the top and we're still struggling to get there."

"Hey mama," April Fools replied, "you've got it." He looked

back at the Seventh Mesa's box. "The least they could do is get themselves reincarnated back to the Third Mesa."

The Great Mother, who had started for the pitcher's mound, quickly spun around. "Then you go down, Mister Fools . . ."

April Fools held up his hands. "Hey baby . . . I'm happy right here with you."

The Whoa Man slapped a new baseball into his glove and positioned their three assistants between him and home plate. "Okay. . . ," he began, as he held up one hand to quiet the crowd. "What's goin' to happen is . . . what we intend to do is create a major polarity between the collective male and The Great Mother's female which will be synthesized by Joe Bamboo into this ordinary baseball. All of this will take place during my lengthy windup. Then, when I feel that all of the necessary power has been generated, I will throw the ball into Nuclear Spud's cyclotronic mind, which, by splitting of the ball's male atoms will create a yang fusion of mass which will then be enlightened by One Hand Clapping as it passes through her Satori." He rubbed one eye and pulled at an ear lobe. "The design is for The Great Mother, who will be at the plate with a Lousiville Laser, to miss the ball." He looked at her. "Therefore, before it crosses the plate it will pass through all of Swiss Army Knife's extended twelve blades."

"Come on, Whoa Man," Porch Swing yelled, "let her hit the ball."

The Whoa Man shook his head and stepped off the pitcher's rubber. "Whoa," he shouted, as he contemplated her demand. "If that were to happen it could create fission instead of fusion which would be a disaster." He rolled his eyes and pulled off his hat. "I mean really big." He walked around the mound and picked up the rosin bag. "With all of its power sucked into the ball, plus all of your auras banging against each other, she's got to miss." Quickly, he looked over at The Great Mother. "You've got to miss, mama."

The Holy Highs looked over at The Heavenites. "Could they possibly be conducting a nuclear experiment?" Buddha Shooting Way asked Moses.

Moses leaned on the rail with his head cradled in one hand. "Partially, I suppose, but then everything is atomic if you understand what I'm saying." He looked over at Mohammed. "God created the Third Mesa that very same way, except that he didn't use a baseball."

"And Darwin whipped God's butt while riding on the back of a giant turtle," April Fools shouted.

Moses laughed. "That could possibly be true, but then Darwin was always such a patient man, and God . . . was exactly the opposite." He clapped his hands. "Instant gratification," he proclaimed, "a true workaholic." He stood up. "I'll make the world in seven days and Darwin will take at least two billion." Moses sat down. "I suppose God was all yang," he said, almost to himself, "and Darwin . . . well he did possess a lot of female intelligence . . . and patience." He looked over at April Fools. "Point well taken, sir . . . and perhaps Darwin should be elevated to Fifth Mesa status. He doesn't fit in with us."

"Hallelujah," Mohammed shouted.

"And Darwin only whipped him in science," The Old Testament added.

The Great Mother picked up her laser bat and tapped each shoe. "You see," she began to explain, as she held the bat into the air for everyone to see, "this bat has been impregnated by lasers with every prayer that has ever been offered for Third Mesa peace. By missing the ball these prayers will act like nuclear bullets which will impregnate The Whoa Man's ball as it passes by me, and if his arm is strong enough, it will be sent out to orbit the Third Mesa."

Moses was shaking his head. "And I thought the Egyptians were weird."

The Great Mother slid her bat underneath her arm and pulled on a pair of batting gloves. "I guess I'm ready . . . Whoa Man."

The Whoa Man tossed the ball into the air and caught it behind his back. "Let's play ball."

Confucius rolled his eyes as he looked up at the cloudless night sky. "I'm confused."

"Hey baby," April Fools yelled over to him, "if you're confusioned about fission, then think how confissioned you could be about fusion." He looked over at The Great Mother and winced. "I'm sorry, mama, I couldn't help myself."

The Great Mother warned him with a straight laced finger pointed from the depth of her eyes. "Hush . . ."

"Just make certain you miss," he said, quietly.

"Ready?" The Whoa Man asked Nuclear Spud.

Nuclear Spud, who looked like a professional wrestler, pounded her gut. "Give me your best shot, Whoa Man babe."

Once again, The Great Mother thumped the bat on home plate. "Here's to peace . . .''

Mohammed leaned over the railing. "What a great field trip we're having."

The Whoa Man received the okay from One Hand Clapping and Swiss Army Knife. He leaned on one knee as if he were searching for secret glyphs from an invisible catcher. The Great Mother stared back, and for a millionth of a second a strange and disturbing thought flashed through her mind. She shook if off and blinked. "Hey," she told herself, "all you have to do, sister, is miss the ball. Don't start getting weird on me, Okay?" Again, she saw The Whoa Man as her adversary. She blinked and looked away. "It's all that collective male energy that's shaking me." She pounded the plate. "Come on, mama, just do your job. Miss it for peace . . . right?"

"Take it downtown, sister."

"You mean Ms it downtown," Thermos corrected.

"Historically," Porch Swing said to the Holy Highs, "that's not what we woman like to do these days." She looked over at them and smiled seductively at Pollen Boy.

He smiled, raised on eyebrow, and turned to his friends. "I would like to take her back with us," he said, "she seems very friendly."

"What?" Confucius shouted. "You've got to be joking. She's only been on the Fifth Mesa a short time."

"Hey baby," April Fools yelled to Pollen Boy, "don't you dare mess with our Porch Swing or your pollen is instant mush."

"Hummm babe," Moses purred to The Whoa Man.

"Atta girl," One Hand Clapping said when she noticed how nervous The Great Mother looked. "Hang in there . . . babe."

The Whoa Man started his windup as he began to attract all of the surrounding male energy into the ball. "Come on you guys, jump on board because we're going for one deep ride within beauty."

The Great Mother cocked the bat.

The Whoa Man's arm looked like a turbo prop at full r.p.m.'s. All of his calculations for the project were travelling through his brain as he concentrated only on becoming one with the ball. "Basically," he thought to himself, "after inventing Beyond Infinity and Mental Orgasms . . . World Peace should be a breeze."

"Got your male on straight," The Great Mother said to the pitcher.

"Gimme five and all of your female compassion baby for we're takin' it on a ride," he answered.

"Peace forever . . . ," she thought, and then let that idea stay within her consciousness.

The banter continued as The Whoa Man's arm, curved-in-time, was rounding Mars and coming home. Nuclear Spud was crouched like a short stop ready for the delivery.

The Whoa Man's mind went back into the Precambrian to gather in some lost ancestors.

The Great Mother smiled for she already had everything she needed.

The Holy People were spanning their seats like granite bridges.

The three Heavenites were amazed that they were having so much fun. Moses jumped onto the back of his seat. "Strike the bum out," he shouted, as he whacked The Old Testament's back. "Look at all that history we thought was lost."

The Old Testament shook his head. "Hey . . . gimme a break, Mo . . . the translators kept throwing out the really good parts."

The Great Mother started to think about all of the good times she had playing hardball with the boys. That wonderful feeling of whacking it out of the park and leaving the boys suspended in their tracks. "Hey!" she suddenly shouted to herself, "jus' miss the ball!"

The Whoa Man was already finished with his windup. Spud's jaws were open and ready. The Great Mother eased off knowing that, being relaxed, she would swing much faster.

"No sweat . . ."

"Humm babe . . ."

And then, there it was. Popping like a collective mind through a fast forward of evolution as it hit the curve of human consciousness—burning through history at the speed of light—to disappear into the Atomic Age of Spud's Potato Mind. The ball's atoms were weighted with the speed of matter, cleaved by the male and swallowed by the female where it was passed on to One Hand Clapping's smiling enlightenment as her Koan satoried it through the temple gate and on to Swiss Army Knife. Blade through blade of polished steel it curved its way through until it passed by the last sentinel.

The Great Mother waited, ondeggiamento.

As patiently as ivory changing into mothers

Leaning in

however, the ball was on an erratic trajectory having been flicked

off course by the last blade which instantly challenged her stance
she had to swing
to protect herself from being struck
rolling her wrists, her shoulders, her hips she struck the ball ripping through her swing to silence that voice within her body. She heard the crack as if everyone's back had been aligned exactly at the same time
heads popped
spectators bolted out of their seats

The Great Mother dropped the bat after her follow through that carried her once around. The Whoa Man collapsed on the mound as he calculated what would happen.

April Fools leaped into the air and pointed at Nuclear Spud. "The ball came out of Spud's Orifice de Waste Hole," he shouted, "I saw it, I saw it, and then it was flicked by Swiss Army Knife's Last Supper Battalion. He ran in front of the box seats. "Wait till next year, folks."

Transfixed, The Holy Highs and Heavenites followed the course of the ball. "I thought she wasn't supposed to hit it," Buddha Shooting Way said.

"I believe we've been tricked by this hocus-pocus of a peace experiment," Moses replied, "and it looks like it's going directly to the moon."

Absentmindedly, The Great Mother started walking toward the mound. "I couldn't help it, Whoa Man," she mumbled, dropping the bat, "it was coming right at me. I had to hit it."

"Just one more fuck-up in the sacred name of science," Nuclear Spud said, as she straightened herself up.

"Hey everyone, don't worry," April Fools yelled. "God can fix it . . . right?" He looked over at the Heavenites. "Right?" The three Heavenites were preparing to leave. "Reverse, reverse," he shouted. He started waving his arms like a cheerleader. "Gimme a R . . . gimme an E . . ."

"Hey!" Thermos shouted, "can't anyone do something?"

"It's all my fault," Swiss Army Knife said to The Whoa Man and The Great Mother. "At the last moment I stuck up my ivory toothpick which caused the ball to veer off course." He shook his head. "I know you had programmed it for only twelve blades."

"No, it's my fault," One Hand Clapping challenged. "I wanted it to be so cosmic that I weighted it down with extra enlightenment."

9

"Hey, all of you knock it off," The Whoa Man shouted, "knock off the guilt." He shrugged, and put his arms around One Hand Clapping and The Great Mother. "I didn't figure in any room for error. That's all. If you want to blame someone, blame me, or our consciousness that makes us want to have a perfect world." He looked up at the moon. "However, we've got a nuclear device about to strike the moon."

There was a long pause as if some powerful force had sucked out everyone's breath. The wind, trees, rivers and crickets were silent. The only sound was the muffled bombardment of the big guns down on the Third Mesa: a soft thumping like a familiar heart beat, Whompf, Whompf, Whompf.

"We blew it," April Fools whispered dramatically to Thermos.

"Can it for once," Thermos yelled, "don't you realize what's happening?"

"Sure I do, but if every day is April Fool's Day, my dear old friend, then what's there to worry about?" He laughed, and started performing cartwheels around the diamond. "April Fools . . . April Fools . . . April Fools," he chanted between flips.

The baseball eventually reached the moon. What followed was an enormous ball of white light that shot horizontally across the moon's face, and then a huge cloud began to build like a giant stretching itself after a long, deep sleep. Rivers of fire crisscrossed the surface until the moon was burning like the sun. Night turned into day, and the Holy People and their guests tried to shield their eyes with anything they could find. Some of them jumped behind the bleachers or fell into the dugouts.

"It's sucking away the oxygen," Nuclear Spud said, as she jumped into the Hall of Famer's box.

April Fools tried to think of something to say, but he was speech-less. "Holy shit," he eventually muttered.

Off in the distance, hundreds of tornados came slicing over the mesa, and then one of them ripped through the stands. Most of the Holy People, and all of the Holy Highs and Heavenites took off for the village as the bleachers were ripped apart. Then, as if in slow motion, the moon exploded. Billions upon billions of particles were shot into space which reflected the sun in diminishing waves of light until there was only darkness. The wind subsided, the stadium lights flickered, went out and came back on.

"My prayers were not in Mama's hot bat," April Fools was fi-

10

nally able to say.

"Or my male energy," Thermos added.

The Whoa Man stepped out of the dugout. "I believe that science, by its very nature, cannot create peace." He made a note in his book. "That, we now understand."

The Great Mother was speechless. She was so confused that her entire body felt numb. All she could do was cry. She couldn't even comprehend what they had tried to do, or even find any justification in the experiment. She had blown up the moon—as if she had just destroyed her own children. Slowly, she stood up, brushed off her clothes, and walked to the edge of the Fifth Mesa where she could look down on the Third Mesa. She sighed and let the tears run down her cheeks. She closed her eyes and took several deep breaths. "What arrogance," she whispered, "what unbelievable arrogance to experiment with something that dangerous." She shook her head as she tried to put what she had done out of her mind. But it wouldn't leave. She was embarrassed, and she didn't want to see anyone. Not that night, the next day, or for a long time. At least, not as The Great Mother. Perhaps she would go down to the Third Mesa and see if there was anything she could do. To help. Something simple. Easy. Nothing more than that. Suddenly, she felt herself almost go into shock as her body began to adjust for the moon's absence. It was a sudden jolt, and then a cold aura came over her that made her feel alone and sick to her stomach. She also stopped crying. She wiped away the tears that had dried like salted crackers on her cheeks and rubbed them with wet grass. There was a moment when she realized that she would never be able to cry again. That emotion went with the moon and she almost felt relieved. She shook her head as she saw the vast panorama around her become only a postcard view: the mountains far away in the background, the deep canyon of Wandering Foot where her son, Kid, was with the children he had stolen, the overpowering sunsets and arrogant sunrises riding over the Third Mesa, the perpetual fireworks show of flares, rockets and missiles going off continually. And somewhere out there was her other son, the warrior, Tuesday Coyote. He too was now only that scenery as if an unbreakable glass shield had somehow been pulled between her and the Third Mesa. Her suffering for humanity had been wiped away as if it were only a mess on a plastic table cloth. She shrugged. "It's only what those Third Mesa people want," she heard herself

11

say. "That's their reality. Why even bother anymore to help them? Perhaps, this was the lesson I had to learn. There's so much that I should be doing to keep the Fifth Mesa safe. Yes, that's what I can do." She looked at her friends. Those old lovers of peace who didn't fit anywhere else except on the Fifth Mesa. Bizarre and eccentric, the dreamers and drifters like The Whoa Man who was much too creative and imaginative for the Heavenites on the Fourth Mesa, and too much of a spiritual renegade for the Seventh. They were all like him. How did April Fools once put it? "Cells dream inside of cells. Laughter is the law to live inside the Fifth Mesa of multiple dimensions where everything is alive, and evolution is the imagination even working on hind tit."

"Yes . . . that's what I'll do. Take care of my own. Help them get shaped up a little so that everything will run more efficiently. Yes, that's definitely the solution."

"Hey!" she called to herself, "you're going to be okay. A little shook up, but you're okay." She patted her face and felt her body. "And . . . just a little fat but still all right for an old lady." She turned toward the Third Mesa. There were fires burning from the night's bombardment. She closed her eyes as she thought how good it was that it was happening down there.

Almost happy, she started walking toward their alpine village. "Tomorrow," she said with a smile, "I'm going to start working out." Once again she examined her body. "A wee bit chunky in places but that can be corrected." She picked up her pace. She was beginning to feel much better as she started to formulate how she would program her days so that she would be more efficient. No dreamer stuff for a long time. Maybe she would even go back to school. That made her laugh and she started to run. "Stay young," she shouted to herself. "That's what you need to do, honey . . . stay young and survive."

April Fools stood alone on the pitcher's mound. "Hey, big mama," he shouted. "Where you going?" She kept on running. He looked at the wrecked stadium. "April Fools," he mumbled. He turned around in a full circle and snapped his fingers. "Hey . . . I said April Fools."

"What did you say?" The Whoa Man asked. He was leaning against the collapsed dugout.

"I said . . . Whoa Man my showman . . . is there any hope for us? Are we crazy or what? Like wanting world peace and then

blowing up the moon. Don't you think that's somewhat weird?''
He walked over to the scientist. "We haven't hurt anyone in our
lives . . . right? That's why we're here. The pacifists' freak show.''
He leaned back against the roof and a heavy shower of dust and
debris fell on them. They didn't seem to notice. "Perhaps you could
spin us through this invention of yours once again, my dear scientist, only this time please do it in reverse." He laughed, and jammed
his hands into his pockets. "If only you could have that one pitch
back. Ha!" He rubbed his hands together and did a quick little jig.
"Fusion, fission, double-humped scission . . . I do believe you made
the wrong division when you nuked big mama's decision.''

"Ahhhh yes," The Whoa Man said in a voice that sounded like
a bloodhound's face. "I think I had way too much yang on the ball.''

"Hey baby, it was way too much of something, that's for sure.''
He pushed himself from the collapsed roof and walked, in measured
acrobatic steps, in a circle. "I'm thinking that we could use a snack
at Dali–Kibbutz's deli." He rubbed his stomach and clapped his
hands three times. "It's time to eat . . .''

"Whoa . . . ," the inventor said softly.

April Fools checked the sky one more time just in case there
had been a mistake, or a bad dream. "April Fools," he said in a low
husky voice. He shrugged and made a large circle with his arms.
"Hey . . . up there . . . it looks like this." He danced around in a large
circle. "I see no moon . . . the moon can't see me," he sang. He
stopped and looked over at The Whoa Man. "I thought for sure both
of you would be immediately promoted to the Seventh Mesa, or
blaze a trail right to the mysterious and Unknown Ninth.''

The Whoa Man joined April Fools as they started toward the
village. "If this had worked," he said, as he turned sideways and
adjusted his cowboy hat, "if this experiment had worked it would
have been a great marriage between science and the humanities . . .
once and for all." He shrugged, and threw away his notebook.

April Fools wrapped his arm tightly around his friend. "I always
thought that April Fool's Day would be a great time to be married.''
He laughed, and squeezed The Whoa Man's arm. "Jus' in case it
didn't work out . . . you understand." He stopped and looked into
the scientist's eyes. "But, it's definitely a much better day for marriages than for world peace experiments. He waved his arms and
started walking backwards. "Or . . . perhaps marriages should be
the only peace experiments allowed." He kicked at a beer can. "How

about that?"

"Whoa," The Whoa Man answered.

April Fools laughed and turned around, "Whoa yourself . . ."

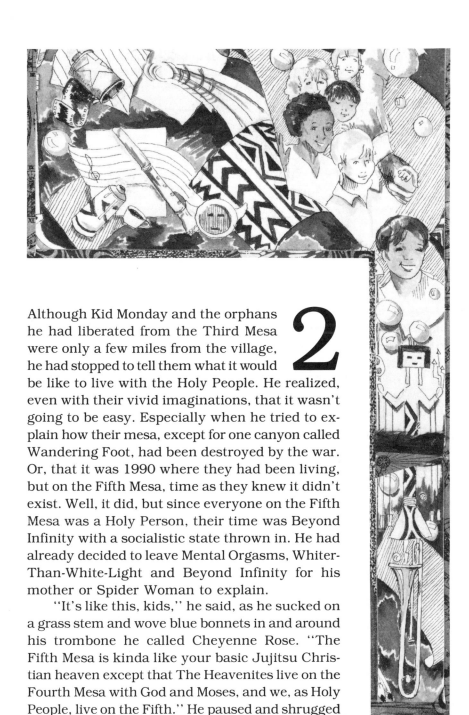

Although Kid Monday and the orphans he had liberated from the Third Mesa were only a few miles from the village, he had stopped to tell them what it would **2** be like to live with the Holy People. He realized, even with their vivid imaginations, that it wasn't going to be easy. Especially when he tried to explain how their mesa, except for one canyon called Wandering Foot, had been destroyed by the war. Or, that it was 1990 where they had been living, but on the Fifth Mesa, time as they knew it didn't exist. Well, it did, but since everyone on the Fifth Mesa was a Holy Person, their time was Beyond Infinity with a socialistic state thrown in. He had already decided to leave Mental Orgasms, Whiter-Than-White-Light and Beyond Infinity for his mother or Spider Woman to explain.

"It's like this, kids," he said, as he sucked on a grass stem and wove blue bonnets in and around his trombone he called Cheyenne Rose. "The Fifth Mesa is kinda like your basic Jujitsu Christian heaven except that The Heavenites live on the Fourth Mesa with God and Moses, and we, as Holy People, live on the Fifth." He paused and shrugged

15

his shoulders. "And everyday is like New Year's with a Native American and Buddhist leitmotif." He paused, as he shook his head and started to laugh at the mess he was making. "Well kids, let me just say that it's something like a Tibetan Halloween party encapsulated in a turbo charged DNA Navajo sandpainting in the Fifth Dimension."

"Yo!" one boy named LaMar, shouted.

"Yo yourself," Kid answered back.

"Tell us about your brother."

"Yeah," one of the older girls added, "tell us again how the two of you made extinct species with some of the female Holy People."

Kid raised his hand. "Whoa there," he yelled, as he threw a handful of grass at them, "you don't need to shout. Holy People have ears just like you."

"Yeah, he's a real Holy Person."

One small girl started to cry and Kid put her on his lap. "I want to go home," she sobbed.

"Sophie," he said as he wiped her cheek and kissed the top of her curly red hair, "you can't go gome because all of the grownups on the Third Mesa have been fighting with each other for so long that soon there won't be anything left."

"I heard that the Holy People are really weird looking," an Indo-Asian boy named Shama said.

Kid laughed, as he reached for the trombone case.

"Yeah, and how come you don't look weird?" the oldest boy named Jamal, asked.

Kid opened up the long black case, took out a large beaded bottle, opened it and examined its contents. The children's eyes got bigger and they started to settle down. "That's because I'm only a first generation Holy Person, but maybe, just maybe, if I really wanted to, I could look just like a bagel with cream cheese."

"That's gross . . ."

"How come you got to be a Holy Person?" Sophie asked.

"Because . . . my old man was a famous wizard named Buddy Sunday, and my mom . . . is . . . The Great Mother. Kid put his trombone together. "Isn't that something?"

"What about your brother?"

"I met him once," the next to oldest boy, La Mar, shouted, "he's a famous warrior."

"That's Tuesday Coyote," Kid said. "His father was Coyote Fats and we have the same mother. In fact . . . we're twins."

"Whoa . . . ," Jamal said, shaking his hands. "I know how that happened."

"Show us with Cheyenne Rose," Shama demanded.

"Yeah, and make some funny cartoons with it," Lisa yelled.

Kid emptied the bottle into the trombone's bell. He was tall, tanned dark and sunbleached wavy blond with a freckled nose. His eyes were a soft jade green, and he had long, graceful hands that seemed to move like musical notes. "Y'know," he said, as he ran the slide back and forth, "I should really be teaching you how the Fifth Mesa works instead of making cartoons out of the Holy People."

"I'm scared," Lisa, the smallest girl said, whose right arm had been amputated. She grabbed Kid's pantleg.

Kid knelt down and put the girl on his knee. "Okay Lisa, let's see if I can conjure up some of these wonderful weirdos." He shook the trombone to make certain the elixir was thoroughly mixed. "Well . . . let me see." He kissed the girl's head. "See . . . actually everyone you'll meet on the Fifth Mesa will look basically just like us . . . very handsome and extremely beautiful." He laughed, and threw a flower at Rosie, the next-to-oldest girl. "But originally most of these people came from other life forms like . . . for instance . . . Joe Bamboo was really a stock of bamboo that was used by the First People to become the Navajo People. And then there's Thermos who at one time was really a thermos bottle. One Hand Clapping was a riddle, or what's called a koan, that is used in Zen Buddhism, and Porch Swing was your basic summer evening's swing on the front porch." He looked at each child to see if they had any questions. "Okay . . . since everything on this planet is alive . . . right . . . just like us . . . these beings evolved into Holy People because of their passionate love for peace." He smiled, and looked up at a pair of falcons that were flying overhead. "That's why they made it to the Fifth Mesa." Again, he kissed Lisa. "And since it was easier for them to communicate by being of the same species, they evolved into your basic human. But, they can change back to their native forms any time they want." Again, he shook the trombone. "It's just like being able to speak two languages."

"Swiss Army Knife's like that?" Juan asked.

"And Beethoven's Fourth Piano Concerto?" Heidi questioned, as she touched Kid's trombone.

"Yeah . . . even they can do that." He put his trombone to his lips, and using only one hand, he blew out a bubble that floated

17

ten feet into the air. It had an iridescent sheen to it and looked up-town all the way. When it reached its full growth it exploded into a highly polished gold film cannister. Kid put down the trombone. "Okay . . . this Holy Person, although she is currently living in a secret monastery on the Fifth Mesa, is an excellent example of Fifth Mesa evolution. She used to be a very famous high fashion model, but after she arrived on this mesa she turned into this roll of devel-oped film. With her gold cover, she moves by continually pulling out the film, looking at each frame with loving admiration, and then winding herself back up. She's called The High Roller."

"Does she always look like that?" Sarah asked, as she cau-tiously walked toward the film cannister.

"Sometimes, when she wants to travel that way, but most of the time she looks just like a normal person." He pointed at Sarah. "In fact, you could be her daughter." Again, he picked up the trom-bone and blew out another bubble. "Now, this one is High Roller's husband." The bubble caught an updraft, rose twenty feet, danced inside a mini-thermal and slowly skidded onto the soft, daisy-flow-ered grass. "He's called Curve Ball . . . and originally he was very famous in many World Series."

"Oh . . . I read about him once," Jamal said.

"I'm sure you did," Kid replied. He blew out nine more bubbles that ended up as miniature Holy People in front of the children. "Now," Kid said, "in real life they are much bigger, but I've con-densed them to be more your size." He looked at the Holy People he had created and then pointed back to Curve Ball. "Okay, with Curve Ball, you'll never really be able to see him. He's only a blur, a swish and then you'll hear a hollow thump as he whaps into an invisible catcher's mitt."

"How was High Roller able to marry someone she couldn't see?"

"Does she ever get balled?" Jamal asked.

All of the kids laughed, even the younger ones who didn't get the joke.

"Well," you've got me there, you guys," Kid replied, as he thought about how mental orgasms were invented to solve such problems. He pointed over to the Holy Person next to Heidi. "That one, Heidi, who looks like a musical score, is Beethoven's Fourth Piano Concerto in . . . ah . . . something A or B or maybe even Z flat." Again, they all laughed. Lisa touched High Roller's gold cannister.

"I know that piece of music," Rosie said.

"Yeah," Jamal added, "it goes like La la la lah lalalala laaaaa."

"Yeah . . . that's exactly right," Kid replied. "Well, she flies around the Fifth Mesa looking like a musical score until she wants to play herself, and then she becomes invisible and only the music can be heard." He scratched his head. "Pretty fascinating . . . right?"

"Who are these others?" Michi asked.

Kid stepped toward the Holy People dressed in their native costumes. "We've got to get going, but tonight, before you go to sleep, they will tell you some bedtime stories about how they became Holy People."

"I want to hear Quarterback Sneak's story," LaMar shouted.

"Yeah . . . and I want to meet Nuclear Spud," Michi added.

"I don't want no scary ones," Lisa said.

"Naw," Kid answered, "it'll be just like watching Saturday morning cartoons without the violence."

"B o r i n g . . . ," Rosie replied, as she looked down the trail. "Hey look!" she shouted, "someone's coming."

Kid looked up and saw a dark-skinned woman walking rapidly up the trail. "That's Spider Woman," he said. Quickly, he put away his trombone. "Come on . . . let's go and meet her."

"What about the Holy People?" Heidi asked.

"Oh yeah," Kid answered. He turned around, clapped his hands twice and they disappeared. "After supper, you'll get to see the real thing."

"She looks like my grandma," one small boy said.

"Spider Woman," Kid said, "was responsible for teaching some of the Third Mesa people the art of weaving." He waved to her.

"I want to look like that someday," Sophie said.

"My mother looks like that," Shama added.

Spider Woman was dressed in a long purple velvet skirt, a dusty rose satin blouse, high deer skin mocassins with silver conchos. Two sheep dogs came bouncing up the trail and when they saw the children they ran into them with yips and juicy face licks.

"Spider Woman," Kid said, as he came up to her, "I was hoping for some reinforcements." He kissed her cheek.

Spider Woman studied Kid's face. "You look tired."

He pulled the kids around him. "We had quite a time trying to sneak out of Wandering Foot." He knelt down and put his arms around as many children as he could reach. "Didn't we?"

"Yeah," Sarah shouted, "the guards were shooting at us and

19

everything."

Spider Woman counted them. "You got them all?"

"Every last one." He stood up. "There were only eleven."

Spider Woman was speechless. She closed her eyes and touched Lisa's face. "That's all?"

"I'm afraid so," Kid answered. "But, I did hear that my brother's wife is alive . . ."

Spider Woman touched Kid's arm. "Your mother's behavior has been very strange lately. That's why I came to see you."

"It's about the moon . . . right?"

Spider Woman nodded. "Yes . . ."

"What happened to the moon?" Heidi asked.

Jamal stepped in closer. "Kid told us that The Great Mother and The Whoa Man blew it up." He looked up at Kid and then over to Spider Woman. "Right . . . ?"

Spider Woman nodded. "They were conducting a peace experiment."

"See . . . Kid was right," Jamal said to LaMar.

Kid put his arm around LaMar's shoulders. "Is she okay?"

"I'm not sure, Kid." She looked at each child and then returned her attention to Kid. Slowly, she started walking toward the village. "She's changed so much." She took Kid's arm. "She's got the community center filled with exercise equipment, the church has been turned into a computer center and she's made the library into a stock exchange." She took Kid's hand. "And listen to this, Kid, she's got The Cowboy Buddha writing her biography."

"Mom's doing all that?"

Juan slipped Kid's trombone out of his hand. "I'll carry this for you." He put it on his shoulder.

"That's right," Spider Woman replied, "your mom."

"Are you two married?" Lisa asked.

Kid laughed, and put his arm around the young girl. "We are in a very spiritual kind of way." He picked her up.

"Kid's got a girl friend at Wandering Foot," she said, as she pulled Kid's nose. "Her name is Molly Rose."

"Why didn't you bring her with you?" Spider Woman asked.

Kid kicked at a rock. "She wouldn't leave. She's a nurse and . . ." He shook his head. "She helped me sneak the kids out of Wandering Foot. Even then, I couldn't convince her to come with us." He sighed, and snuggled his face against Lisa's hair. "She doesn't belong down there, Spider Woman, and I'm really worried that something is going to happen to her."

"That's too bad," Spider Woman replied, as she took Lisa out of his arms. "However, I believe that your mother has some news about your brother."

"Really?"

Spider Woman nodded. "Why don't you run on ahead and I'll stay with the kids."

Kid reached over and lifted his trombone from Juan's shoulder. "I'd better keep this with me . . . Juan." He started to walk backwards. "You guys be good to Spider Woman and I'll come with some of the Holy People later on."

"You'd better . . ."

"Don't worry, I will." He waved, and then started to run down the trail.

"Do you know Molly Rose?" Lisa asked Spider Woman.

"No . . . do you?"

"Yes, and she nursed me back alive when I was knocked dead by a big bomb." She lifted up her skirt and showed Spider Woman a long scar that ran across her stomach. "See . . . some glasses cut me."

"Is that when you met Molly?"

"Yes, and my brother Kelly died, and my dog and my grandfather too."

Spider Woman kissed her cheek. "I'm so very sorry." She turned and faced the children as she tried to touch as many of them as she could. "And I'm so very pleased that you got out of Wandering Foot. So very, very happy." She put Lisa down but kept a hold of her hand.

"I love Molly, too," Sophie said, "and I love Kid because he's so funny."

"Everybody loves Kid," Spider Woman answered, "and the best thing is that he loves everybody right back." Spider Woman stopped as they rounded a bend in the alpine trail. "Look, there's the Holy People's village."

"Oh golly . . . it's so beautiful."

"Look at the big mountains," Heidi shouted.

"And there's still snow on them," Rosie exclaimed, as she raced down the trail. "Yipppeeee . . ."

"That's why all of the buildings are made out of big logs with

21

steep roofs," Spider Woman said, as she started walking. "Come on kids, we'll be there in just a few minutes."

"Where's Kid?" the youngest girl asked.

"He went to see his mother."

"Is she really The Great Mother?"

Spider Woman paused as she counted the children who had stayed with her. "Yes . . ."

"Wow, that really must be fantastic," Sophie said.

Spider Woman grabbed Lisa's hand to keep her from falling. Two more kids took off for the village. Smoke was coming out of the chimneys, and some of the Holy People were walking up the trail to meet them. A Tasmanian owl flew overhead and landed in a Yew pine.

"How come The Great Mother blew up the moon?" Heidi asked.

"Because . . . she . . . ah . . . for just one moment stopped being The Great Mother," Spider Woman answered. She looked into the sky for the evening star.

"What does that mean?" Heidi questioned.

Spider Woman closed her eyes as she saw The Great Mother swing at The Whoa Man's ball. "I think . . . my dear, she reacted."

The girl stopped and looked into Spider Woman's eyes. "That's exactly what Molly would have said."

Spider Woman smiled as she pulled Molly's face out of her imagination. "That's good," she replied, as she once again picked up Lisa. "I think I'm really going to like that Molly girl."

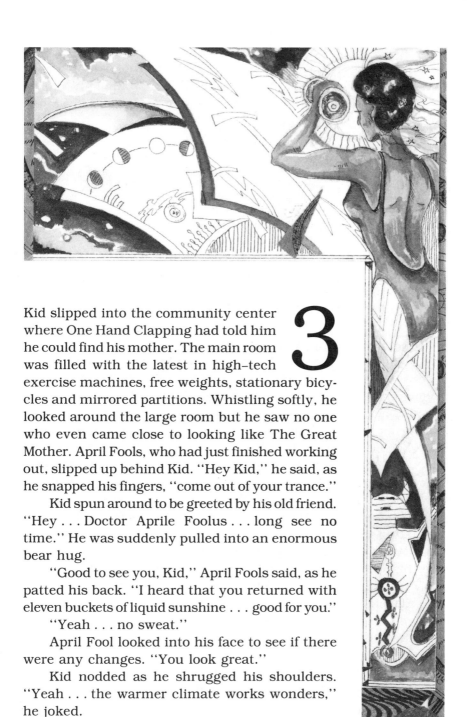

Kid slipped into the community center where One Hand Clapping had told him he could find his mother. The main room was filled with the latest in high-tech exercise machines, free weights, stationary bicycles and mirrored partitions. Whistling softly, he looked around the large room but he saw no one who even came close to looking like The Great Mother. April Fools, who had just finished working out, slipped up behind Kid. "Hey Kid," he said, as he snapped his fingers, "come out of your trance."

Kid spun around to be greeted by his old friend. "Hey . . . Doctor Aprile Foolus . . . long see no time." He was suddenly pulled into an enormous bear hug.

"Good to see you, Kid," April Fools said, as he patted his back. "I heard that you returned with eleven buckets of liquid sunshine . . . good for you."

"Yeah . . . no sweat."

April Fool looked into his face to see if there were any changes. "You look great."

Kid nodded as he shrugged his shoulders. "Yeah . . . the warmer climate works wonders," he joked.

"Have you seen your mom?"

Kid shook his head, "No . . . I've been looking for her."

April Fools seemed surprised. He spun Kid around and pointed his body at a young looking woman who was pumping furiously on one of the bicycles. A towel was hanging around her neck and she was fashionably outfitted in brightly colored tights, leg warmers, leotards and a red silk headband. "That, my dear young friend, is . . . your mama."

Kid stared as he rocked back and forth. "Ah . . . come on . . ."

"Tis true m'lord."

"That's my mother?"

One Hand Clapping walked over to them. "Doesn't she look hot?"

"Yo," Kid replied softly, as he slowly stepped toward the person who was supposedly his mother. One Hand Clapping went over to the fireplace to build a fire.

April Fools stayed behind Kid. "Great body . . . heh?"

Kid was speechless. He stopped, looked over at April Fools to see if he was being put on and then took another step. What he was seeing wasn't anything like he had ever known, and he couldn't believe the transformation. The Great Mother's long legs looked as if they diminished five octaves above her feet. She was tall, dark skinned, her eyes were large and her silver gray hair was trimmed close to her head. She had broad shoulders, a long neck and smooth lineal body that moved like an Italian racing car. She changed over to the quadraceps machine, and locked in her ankles. Joe Bamboo took over the bicycle. The Great Mother looked up and noticed her son. "Hey Kid . . . !" she shouted.

Kid hung back as he examined this stranger's face in hopes of discovering something that reminded him of his mother. Joe Bamboo started pumping as fast as he could to impress Kid's mother. Kid stuck his hands in his coat pockets and bit his lower lip. "Mom . . . ?"

"Did you get the kids?" she asked, as if nothing had changed.

"Eleven," he replied. He sat down on the edge of a leather-covered bench. "That's all there were." He looked over at the lats machine and saw The Whoa Man working out. "Looks like everyone's gettin' physical."

"How do I look?" she asked between breaths.

Kid cocked his head and shrugged. "I liked you better when you looked like Aunt Jemima."

24

"What a horrid thing to say," she replied. She stopped working out and studied Kid's face. "You look beat."

Spider Woman, who had just come into the room, stopped at the bench. "What do you think?"

Kid closed one eye and looked over at Spider Woman. Somewhere riding through his heart he had this feeling of a wonderfully large, bouncy woman with large breasts, thighs and shoulders who could carry the planet and push galaxies out of the way when defending her young. She was also graceful, an incredible cook, played a mean game of Five Card Stud, loved baseball, wrote lead sheets for her musician friends, drank like a fish and could whip out a five course breakfast for the baseball team before prayer meeting. But this, this skinny ass'd pornographic angel could be his graduation date. How was he ever going to relate to her? This anti-mom. "I think," he said softly, "I'm flabbergasted."

His mother moved over to the slant board, set the angle at a much stiffer pitch and locked in her feet. Upside down, she looked at her son, "Change, and I'll run you through the machines."

Kid slapped his trombone case, "Naw, I think ol' Cheyenne Rose and I'll go over to the deli and stuff ourselves with burgers and fries." He looked over at Spider Woman and winked.

"Yuk," The Great Mother yelled, as she quickly went through thirty sit-ups.

Spider Woman touched Kid's arm. "I was over at the communication center and they've got some new information about your brother."

"What?" Kid excitedly asked. "Where is he?"

Spider Woman took his hand. "Your mother has all of this information, ask her." She kissed his cheek. "I've got to run," she said, as she stood up. "Leonardo is cooking supper. Would you like to join us?"

"Naw," he answered, "I'm just going to hang out here." He motioned toward his mother. "I think there was a mix-up at the hospital. He laughed and stood up. "Besides, I'm going over to check on the kids." He kissed her. "What's all this communication center talk?"

"Satellites and computers, Kid. We now know everything." She raised one eyebrow and rolled her eyes. She stepped closer. "Truthfully, I think we lost all of our telepathic skills when the moon was blown up." She looked over at The Great Mother. "Now, we can check out all of the different mesas, night or day."

"That's how she found out about Tuesday . . . right?"

She nodded. "I've got to run."

Kid waved, and walked over to the bench where his mother was pressing two hundred pounds. "What have you found out about Tuesday?" He tried to look into her eyes. "Remember him . . . your son?"

The Great Mother slipped the bar onto the rack and took a deep breath. "Listen Kid, I've changed my name."

Kid looked at the beamed ceiling and blinked. He didn't even want to respond. He wanted to hear about his brother, or how she and The Whoa Man blew up the moon. He couldn't figure out her coolness. It was as if she had emotionally detached herself from the world. He straddled the bench and sat on her stomach. "Okay . . . I want the truth . . . Mom."

"Get off me you big galute."

He lifted up his legs so all of his weight was on her. "Who's that in there?" he asked, as he poked at her rib cage. She bucked up and he pulled himself away. "I think an anorexic Lamborghini has invaded your body."

She wiped her face with her pink towel. "Listen Kid, I'm sick and tired of being The Great Mother." She threw the towel at him. "Have you any idea what a drag that is? She took off her headband. "Well I can tell you, Kid . . . it's a big fucking drag."

"That's why you sent me down to rescue the Third Mesa children . . . ?" he asked, "because it's such a drag?" He threw the towel back at her.

"So . . . we've got the kids." She smelled the towel and threw it on the ground. "I'm happy for them, but they're your responsibility. Or Spider Woman's."

Kid shrugged. "Yeah . . . sure . . . whatever you say."

"I'm going to start school in the Fall." She leaped onto the bicycle. "I've had it with this mother moon crap."

Kid couldn't believe what he had just heard. He wanted to ask her if she was on drugs. The fire was roaring in the petrified wood fireplace, and the room smelled of sweat, perfume and pine pitch. Swiss Army Knife was putting the moves on One Hand Clapping. Kid stood up. "What's your new name?"

"Mona," she answered.

Kid closed his eyes. "Just Mona?"

"Should there be more?" she answered. "Do you know any other woman on the Fifth Mesa named Mona?" She set the resistance on the bicycle as high as it would go.

"Well, gosh," Kid answered, facetiously, with a country accent, "I guess I really don't know thar . . . Mona." He waved to Dali–Kibbutz when she came in to work out. She blew him a kiss. "When I was crossing the desert on the Third Mesa, I met some renegade soldiers who would give anything to whisper sweet nothings into Mona's ear."

Mona clapped her hands as she continued to pedal. "That's exactly what I need to hear," she replied. "Snap heads around, devastate them with my soon-to-be brilliant mind and leave them high and dry begging for more." She began to pump. "Just how much would they give?" she asked.

"Well, darn ma'am, I guess they'd jus' 'bout be willin' to give up two packs of freeze dried camel dung cigarettes," Kid answered.

Mona scoffed, as she stood up to pedal. "You sound like your brother."

Kid picked up Mona's headband and twirled it on his fingers. It smelled of sweat and perfume. It made him feel frightened because it was so sexy. He walked over to the dumb bell rack and picked up two twenty-five pounders. "Well Mona," he said, as he stretched out the vowels in her new name as far as they would go. "Spider Woman told me you've got some news about Tuesday." He lifted the weights and put them back on the rack. "You know, my younger brother of three minutes who has been gone from the Fifth Mesa for ten years."

Mona jumped off the bike and posed in front of the mirror. "Tuesday Coyote," she answered as she picked up two ten-pound dumb bells, "your brother is on his way to Wandering Foot to find his wife." She lifted the weights from both sides of her body.

Kid took off his coat and shirt and pretended to be examining his muscles. "What else do you know about him?" He struck a pose. "Hey, hey, hey . . ."

A log in the fire cracked. April Fools came over pretending to be Ground Hog's Day.

"Your brother has been fighting against the women, he has a serious leg wound, he drinks too much, he's been heavily into opium, he's been separated from his wife for eight years and he hasn't made love with another woman since."

27

Kid laughed. "Billions of dollars worth of equipment and that's all you found out?" He picked up two five-pound dumb bells. "Just think, back in the olden days all Mesa Fivers could communicate with their noses." He quickly went through five reps with the weights. "Sniff 'em out." He looked over at his mother. "I want to know how his heart is doing . . . Mona. How his soul is, and if he's found what he's been looking for. And you give me secret police bullshit." He began to furiously lift the weights. "Ladeeeees and Genneldubs . . . here is Mesa Five's most amazing kidnapper, dildo head, bon vivant and left-handed masterbater, attempting to break the world's stupidity record by thinking of nothing while lifting these weights eighty-five trillion times, grandisonante. And since Mesa Fivers can feed themselves osmotically, he has put a giant box of Wheaties and two quarts of milk into his old, broken down cowboy boots, and will feed himself through the soles of his feet." He looked into the mirror, shook his head and sat down. "My brother hasn't made love for eight years?"

Mona nodded—frozen in a pose to define her latissimus dorsi muscles.

"Yo . . . ," he said softly, "that doesn't sound like my brother." Kid began to reminisce about when they had discovered a way to recreate extinct species. It made him happy and it felt like a huge, fat smile was running the one hundred meter dash up his spine.

"What's so funny?" his mother asked.

Kid stretched out on the bench. "You, me, the world." He closed his eyes and took a deep breath. "I'm in love, Mom." He turned his head toward his mother. "I suppose you already know about that?"

Mona jumped off the bike and checked her abdomen in the mirror. "I know."

"So . . . ?"

"Her father was a dumb cowboy."

Kid sat up. "That's not true," Kid challenged. "Her step-father was a famous rodeo star, but her real father was a Tibetan shaman, and her mother was an Apache freedom fighter."

Mona turned toward her son. "Kid, we've got years and years of history as Holy People." She sat down on the bench. "Think about that."

"Who thinks when you're in love," Kid answered. He smiled and felt her right arm. "You know who said that?"

Mona stood up. "It sounds like something your father would

28

have said."

Kid laughed, as he picked up his trombone. "You said it . . . ah . . . Mona . . . when you told me about my dad . . . who just happened to be an itinerant wizard rodeo boy with . . . how did you put it . . . 'the sweetest face this side of Mesa Seven's halos.'" He rubbed his forehead and put the case over his shoulder. "And not only that . . . you got yourself into one of those haystack threesomes with my ol' man and Coyote Fats to boot." He laughed, and his eyes looked as if two neon lights had been turned on. "You used to talk about it all of the time . . . with great joy."

"That was a long time ago . . . Kid," she answered, as she examined her deltoid muscles.

"Hey . . . not only did you brag about it, but it also got you two twins with separate fathers." Kid started to walk away, but turned back. "And you told Spider Woman that you'd love to do it again."

Mona spun around with her hands on her hips. "If you're still looking for a mother, I'm sure Spider Woman will be more than happy to accommodate you."

Kid was stunned. Absentmindedly, he patted his trombone. "Okay . . . ," he replied, as he started to back away, "are you sure you don't want to have a couple of burgers with me?"

Mona watched her son back away. "How about jogging with me in the morning?"

Kid shook his head. He wanted to tell her that he was going back to the Third Mesa, but he couldn't find the words. Of course, he thought to himself, he would tell Spider Woman and Leonardo. He swallowed a lump in his throat and sniffed. "No . . . I don't think so Mona," he replied, "because that would also include a high colonic coffee enema while jogging backwards through five reincarnations." He laughed. Mona was back on the bicycle. He slapped the case. "Okay . . . see you later . . ."

Mona bounced over to a large music consol, flipped a switch and instantly the room was filled with aerobic music. She did three spins, dropped into the splits, rolled over and powered her body into a handstand.

Kid stood watching her in the doorway. "Lookin' good, Mama Mona," he said, as he flipped out a thumb. "Aunt Jemima could never do that." He opened the door and stepped out. "But then, she never blew up the moon . . . either."

General Tuesday Coyote drove his old military truck to the edge of a deep valley and looked down into the gorge that was filled with terraced lakes, water-falls, countless streams spilling off high red sandstone walls. A river of pure water, having its headwaters on the Fifth Mesa, dropped from the upper falls into the fertile canyon. A layer of morning mist had settled over the lakes. As he stepped to the edge it felt exactly the same as when he and his wife, Ava Matisse, helped build the Japanese-styled gardens and residences as a sanctuary for war refugees. Later on, it was taken over and turned into a military camp for the women's army led by General May Liberty. When that happened, Coyote took off and joined the men's army; Ava stayed and fought with the women. It had been a hard defeat for him, but now, as he returned after many years of being out in the desert, the village looked almost exactly the same: the first oasis within a thousand miles.

Behind him, there was a vast desert that was so desolate only hardened veterans who knew the old roads would dare enter. It was filled with burned military aircraft, blown-up trucks, jeeps, tanks, spent missiles, poisonous snakes, skeletons and the remains of the male army. The desert was truly a no-man's land where only a few mad souls were able to take it on.

Coyote reached into his shirt pocket and took out an envelope that contained a letter from Molly Rose. He had already memorized the message, but he needed the reassurance that he would be able to find her once he arrived at Wandering Foot. It had been years since he had seen her, and many times he had heard that she had been killed while working as a nurse. He opened the letter and studied the calligraphy as if it were a foreign language. He rode with the swells and valleys of each character, taking the ride through the dark tunnels, almost begging for something more. For the fifth time that day he read the letter.

> *Dear Tuesday (You'll never be a General to me),*
>
> *I've been sending you my special telepathic mojo messages for the past month, but I guess you're too old and worn out to pick up on them. Therefore, you old fart, I'm sending you this kind if you haven't forgotten how to read . . . which serves you right for being such a big shot general and fighting against the women. I also heard that you've defected and you're on your way here to find Ava. There were rumors that she was here, but I've been kept in the dark because I refuse to fight. That's General May Ironpants Liberty for you. The old bitch!!! Please be careful for I'm afraid she might try and do you in like she's done in so many men who have ended up here. Don't worry about finding me, because I'll know when you show up. You just have that Fifth Mesa smell about you.*
>
> > *Yours truly,*
> > *Molly Rose*
>
> *P.S. Your beautiful twin was here and stole all of the kids plus my heart. Hurrah! I'm in love. Hot stuff . . . heh? Please take care and be careful.*

Coyote felt a faint glow of hope as he carefully folded the letter and returned it to his pocket. He stepped onto a point of land and looked into the canyon. The sun, breaking over Double Lightning Plateau left everything in shadows. Still, he could see it the way it had been before he left—this Shangri-la riding in buffalo moons, meditation gardens, reflecting pools—with all of the trees, shrubs, plants and lanterns that he and Ava had brought back from Japan.

It had all happened before the war. Before they had taken sides and he had left Wandering Foot. When they were working side by side with the gardeners and carpenters from Japan. It had been so peaceful and they had been so close. They were also skydivers, and occasionally they would enter as many events as they could with high hopes of winning some extra money. One year, they won first place. The trophy was as tall as they were, and the prize money seemed like a fortune. Now, as he watched the light slowly moving down the canyon walls, the sanctuary seemed like a ship lost at sea—an anomaly to everything that had brought about its creation.

He found the secret road that led into the canyon, put the old truck into compound low and prayed for the brakes to hold. As he passed under the first waterfall he could feel the desert slowly being washed away. That was how Wandering Foot had always been, and he was amazed that it was still possible.

After seven miles of switchbacks, he finally arrived at the last water-fall. He stopped the truck, removed his worn-out khaki clothes and threw himself into the deep pool below the falls. When he surfaced he noticed a silk kimono and sandles had been laid out for him on a wooden bench. He looked around but could not see anyone. The vegetation was so dense that someone could be hiding only a few feet away. He turned his back and remained in the water until he felt that he had rid his body of the alkali dust that came from crossing the vast desert.

The deep green pool reminded him so much of Ava's cool spirit, and his thoughts went back to when he first met her. He had been working on the main villa at Wandering Foot when he noticed a woman folded in a perfect lotus on the opposite side of the river. Wild revolutionary hair, a skin that sparkled with a mother-of-pearl iridescence, the softest of a smile, a body that was kind to itself. Coyote put down his tools, bowed to the master carpenter, and walked out into the garden to try and bring his body back into some kind of control. Ava, who had been watching Coyote, followed him through the main gate and found him bathing in the deep pool below the falls. They smiled. She removed her clothes as he watched in silence. At that moment, it felt to them that everything had suddenly been given away and they were ready to accept that gift. Whatever it was that had caused them to find each other needed to be explored.

Coyote slipped carefully out of the water and dried himself under a Kuroganemochi tree, recently blossomed with white fragrant flowers. He put on the kimono and slipped into the sandals. He looked back at the old truck that had carried him through the desert, waved in admiration, and then took what he remembered as the stone path that led to the large wooden gate a mile down river.

He felt as though he was being watched, but he was so enchanted by the remaining landscape, the serene beauty of the flowers, the blossoming camelia trees, that for moments at a time he would forget about the pain in his leg, the fact that he had deserted his own army, or that he had run out of opium the week before. And then, when he came to, he would begin to question his motives for giving up. If everything was eventually going to go, he would be much more comfortable in the desert. He saw his get-up in one of the pools that was formed by an underground spring. He felt silly and he wished he had kept his old clothes. When he came to the first stone bench he took some water from the laver with a bamboo ladle. He unshouldered his pack and sat down. Inside the leather and canvas bag he had a machine gun, two pistols and one hundred rounds of ammo. Plus, an old flask that held a pint of brandy. It was all he had left. Everything else, he thought to himself, was inside, and there wasn't much of that. At twenty-seven, it seemed as if there was another century tacked on. He stared at the weapons and remembered when the war refugees would arrive on the same trail. He took a deep breath and slowly, with puffed cheeks, released the air. He looked at a maple tree and in each slender leaf he saw Ava's tracks, and in the shimmering light, her smile. That's why he was coming in. He had to keep reminding himself. Yes, that's it. He picked up his pack and it felt so much heavier than before. Like an old, grouchy friend, it had been a part of him for so long. He shuddered at its eight years of being his survival. Quickly, he buried it behind a stone lantern that looked like an ancient sentinel. He wrapped the flask in a large piece of cloth and tied it around his waist. "I've given up," he said out loud. "No one was right and everyone was dead wrong." He started walking. "Happily delusioned by truth."

When he arrived at the large hand-carved wooden gate, a quiet shiver teased through his body and he remembered a saying by Zeami Motokiyo, the author of the Noh Theater. He allowed it to run through his mind as he walked on the circling path that took him in the direction of the first lake. *To watch the sun sink behind a flower-clad hill, to wander on and on in a huge forest with no thoughts of return, to stand upon the shore and gaze after a boat that has gone beyond the islands, to ponder on the journey of wild geese and lost among the clouds.*

He strolled around the first lake as his eyes sought the reflection of the clouds on the surface of the water with the flashing colors of the koi swimming below. "Heaven and earth, equally balanced, and indistinguishable," he thought to himself. "The infinity of nature held within the finiteness of cupped hands holding the perfect universe."

He ducked behind a tall stone lantern when he spotted two women guards coming his way. They were dressed in fatigues, and he suddenly felt very sad as he watched them walk away. They were both young and they made him think back to when he and Ava were building the gardens and houses. He looked at his body in the reflecting pond and he saw an old man who could hardly beg an image.

Leaving the akusuga-doro, he came to a path that took him toward the river. Crossing over a stone zigzag bridge he passed through a double hedge of blooming azalea trees, and emerged at a secluded pond surrounded by his favorite trees: Torch Azaleas, Sasanqua Camelia, Cape Jasmine, and Heavenly Bamboo. The jasmines were just beginning to bud. Three granite boulders faced him on the other side of the water. Coyote sat down next to an anise tree and tucked his legs, with much difficulty, into a half-lotus. Once he was able to make himself comfortable, he began to absorb the delicate scents from the plants. It felt to him as if he was slowly being lifted away from the earth.

Somewhere, off in the distance, the whack of a Sozu broke into his meditation as its noise refocused his attention. It was a long bamboo pipe that when filled with water from a smaller pipe, tilted from the added weight and emptied itself. When the water spilled out, it swung back to its receptive position and struck a rock. It worked as a transcending pulse, and soon he had slipped into a dream about the moon. It was a common dream since it had been his only woman for so many years. Both sides blamed each other, but then he discovered that his mother and The Whoa Man were responsible. How could that be? There hasn't been any violence, or even intentions of violence on the Fifth Mesa for thousands of years. Perhaps, he mused, with his brother's help, they just might be able to create a new one. Or, better yet, they just might be able to steal one of Saturn's many moons. It almost made him laugh.

After some time, he felt a delicate shadow pass over him, and he slowly opened his eyes and looked into the face of Molly Rose. "Are you the moon?" he asked softly, squinting to see her head encircled by a nimbus of light that eclipsed the morning sun.

Molly sat down, tucked her legs underneath her kimono and bowed, ever so slightly. "The moon is travelling the lost highway, and I am, unfortunately, only its shadow."

Coyote reached over and gently took Molly's hand as he watched her face. "Molly, you are truly the seventh sunrise, and everything else in this world is . . . your shadow."

Molly blushed. Her Eurasian face was open and full like a single flower. He had known her since the day she was born. Tibetan father, Apache-Anglo mother—to his eyes she was like a healing sandpainting. Her long black hair was tied up braids with a camelia blossom pinned over her right ear. She moved in closer as she felt his happiness upon seeing her. "I'm so glad you're here."

"How are you?" he asked.

She hesitated, and Coyote could see from her eyes that she had something to tell him. "I think I have some good news, Coyote."

"Ava?" The Sozu struck the rock exactly when he said his wife's name.

"Yes, and from what I've been able to find out, she might be here at Wandering Foot." She touched his arm. "Be careful."

"Ava," he repeated. He looked across the pond at a lantern which seemed to be laughing. He sighed. "Is she all right?"

"I don't know," Molly answered. "As the soldiers keep telling me, I'm only a simple nurse. Way below their status as a mighty warrior." She laughed, as she looked into Coyote's eyes. "Kid was here a few weeks ago. He took all the children with him to the Fifth Mesa."

"Yo," Coyote answered, as a smile almost broke across his sunburned face. "How is he?"

36

"Beautifully crazy."

"I'll just bet ol' ironpants Liberty would like to nail his ass."

"She hasn't even figured out why he did it." Molly said, as she touched Coyote's hands. "She's a mean one, Coyote." She rubbed his fingers. "Watch out."

"That's okay, Molly. She can't do anything to me." He touched her hand. "I just want to find Ava and eventually head back home."

"To the Fifth Mesa?"

He nodded. "And you should get out of here because what's left of the men's army will soon be attacking Wandering Foot. They don't have much, but I can assure you they mean to get this place." He looked around the enclosure. "This is it, right here."

"General Liberty won't give it up."

Coyote shrugged. He looked into Molly's dark eyes. "You love Kid don't you?"

"Yes," she answered shyly. She looked at her feet and then slowly raised her eyes. "He's so . . . kind."

"Everybody loves Kid." He shook his head and bit his lower lip. "We were so different." Coyote studied his hands as he wagged his head. "He took everything so easily, and I . . ."

"Kid talks about you all of the time." Molly looked around when she heard voices on the other side of the enclosure. She waited until the sounds diminished. She turned back. "I know everything you guys did together, even your ceremonial peeing contests."

Coyote squinted and furled his brows. "I can't remember."

"Kid does. He remembers everything. He loves you more than you will ever know, Coyote."

Coyote remained silent for a long time. "He was like having a golden retriever for a brother." He laughed and leaned back on his hands. "And I . . . I was the pet coyote gone wild." He watched a hawk ride a high thermal. "Look, there's my guardian."

Molly looked up to watch the raptor. They were silent for what seemed to be a century of peace and silence—until they heard the sounds of exploding shells up on the rim. Molly rocked up on her knees. "I should get back to the hospital." She stood up. "You can stay at my place," she said, as she helped Coyote up.

Coyote tried out his bad leg. "I'll just go find General Liberty," he replied. "I have nothing to lose."

"Be careful . . ."

"I've seen it all, Molly," He looked into her eyes and then quickly lowered them. "She can have me if she'll turn Ava loose."

"Yikes," Molly replied.

"I don't think she's interested in doing much to this old sinewy hunk of rawhide." There was another barrage of shells. "They're getting closer."

"Come on then," Molly replied, "I'll take you there. That might help." She took his hand. "For some reason she still likes me."

Coyote snickered as he put his arm around her shoulders. "Because she knows that kid's got a fancy for you."

"That would be awful."

"It all is, Molly . . . it all is."

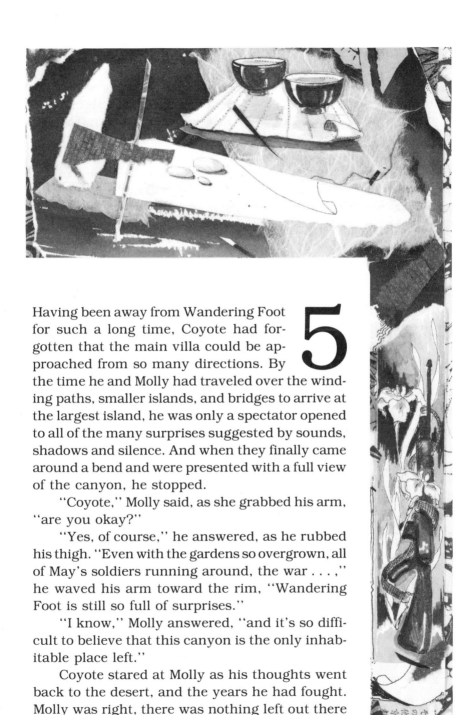

Having been away from Wandering Foot for such a long time, Coyote had forgotten that the main villa could be approached from so many directions. By **5** the time he and Molly had traveled over the winding paths, smaller islands, and bridges to arrive at the largest island, he was only a spectator opened to all of the many surprises suggested by sounds, shadows and silence. And when they finally came around a bend and were presented with a full view of the canyon, he stopped.

"Coyote," Molly said, as she grabbed his arm, "are you okay?"

"Yes, of course," he answered, as he rubbed his thigh. "Even with the gardens so overgrown, all of May's soldiers running around, the war . . . ," he waved his arm toward the rim, "Wandering Foot is still so full of surprises."

"I know," Molly answered, "and it's so difficult to believe that this canyon is the only inhabitable place left."

Coyote stared at Molly as his thoughts went back to the desert, and the years he had fought. Molly was right, there was nothing left out there

39

except the male psyche gone mad from desperation until it finally pulled the female in with it. And ironically enough, all that was left was this earth's opening—the passageway to the Fifth Mesa—the only clean water fed through miles of aquifer from his homeland. If the Holy People ever stopped the water it would be all over for Wandering Foot. A smile cracked through his saddened face. "It was such a fleeting moment of beauty when we helped put this place together. This retreat. When I was digging ditches, sweating like a hog, and working twelve to sixteen hours a day, Ava kept reciting this one saying from somewhere, I can't remember, but it went something like, 'Welcome the stranger for that person might have lived with angels.'" Coyote shook his head and kicked at a leaf that had fallen onto the path. "We had high hopes which for me was really something."

"And now?" Molly asked.

They continued walking. "I'm worn out." He touched Molly's face. "I just kicked a grizzly of an opium habit, I still need hooch, my liver is like a dead lake, and . . . ," he closed his eyes. "I would like to have a kid someday, but I . . . ah . . . haven't been able to make love for years." He emitted a laughing grunt, and rolled his eyes. "I'm one of the lucky ones, they say."

"Oh Coyote," Molly replied, as she openly wiped away a tear, "Kid told me that you treated life as if it was your enemy."

"Peace was the enemy," he said flatly. They came to the entrance to the main villa. "It bored me." He smiled and stopped so he could look into her eyes. "Kid flourished with it and I died." He shook his head. "Figure that one out."

Molly studied Coyote's hardened face. "Are you ready for this?"

"I'm not sure."

"You could rest before your meeting. I'm sure that would be all right."

"Maybe that would be better."

"There's a guest room in the villa. I'll go see about using it," Molly answered. They passed through the courtyard and stopped at the kutsunuginishi—the shoe taking-off stone. Coyote was surprised that Molly didn't stop but continued on. Two of General May's bodyguards were standing behind the sliding glass doors.

*   *   *   *   *

Coyote stared at the bamboo ceiling and circular fan. Three times

40

a dragontail butterfly flew in through the open window, patroled the guest room and easily escaped. With each visit, it seemed to Coyote that he felt quieter and more relaxed. Once, he thought that his brother might be sending him messages, but he shook it off as too much nonsense. Maybe it was Ava? All he wanted was a few hours of sleep but none came. Around six-thirty he dozed off only to be awakened at seven for his meeting with General Liberty. He took a bath, shaved, put on a clean kimono. As he examined himself in front of the mirror, he took a long pull of brandy from the flask. He didn't know what he would do when he ran out. Quit, or make his own, and he realized that it would be much easier to do the latter. If necessary he would make it out of rusted steel.

General Liberty was waiting for him on the veranda. Two of her bodyguards were standing in front of the fusuma and Coyote could see two more on the other side of the sliding doors.

"General Coyote," the woman said, as she took two steps down the stairs.

Coyote accepted her hand without taking his eyes away from her face. Even in military dress she remained beautiful. He cautioned himself that she still had a deceiving beauty that could stand almost every male up on his libido. Another dragontail, or perhaps the same one, suddenly dropped from a maple tree. "General Liberty," he answered, "I'm no longer a general of anything . . . especially the military."

"Ahhhh . . . another born again."

Coyote had always thought of May as having four heads, and the one she seemed to be wearing that evening made him more nervous than the others. "I am just that," he answered.

"Tea?" she asked, as she turned to accompany him inside. The sliding glass screens were opened and then the shojis. Coyote followed May into one of the smaller tea rooms, and, as custom, took the seat on the guest mat. Although the idea for the tea room was originally designed to leave behind worldly concerns, he couldn't help feel that this was not going to be the case. May said something to the attendant in the preparation chamber and then sat down on the nobleman's mat.

Listening to the water boil, observing the single flower in the alcove's vase, absorbing the simplicity of the room's rustic interior, Coyote vowed that he would obey the ceremony and give in to the calling of the room. Smiling, he looked up from his thoughts. "I'm

41

looking for my wife, Ava Matisse.''

May accepted Coyote's statement in silence. An attendant came in, poured hot water into a dark ceramic pot, and knelt down to wait for the tea to steep. "I assumed, Mister Coyote, perhaps that was one of your reasons for coming in." She looked at her attendant who was in her late teens and dressed in fatigues. "However, your wife is not at Wandering Foot, and I have not heard anything about her for a long time."

Coyote studied her face for any sign that she just might be lying. She seemed sincere, but then, he thought, why wouldn't she be, lying or not. He took a deep breath and let it slowly ease out of him as he tried not to lose hope. "I heard from a reliable source that she was here."

"You heard wrong." The tea was passed. Holding the cup with two hands, May tasted the light green liquid. "However, I am very concerned that your brother, Kid Monday, has taken our children." She tried to smile but it fit her face like a bird's broken wing. "I might be able to find out where your wife is, assuming that she is alive, if you can persuade your brother to bring back our children."

I haven't seen my brother for years, General, and besides, I have no control over him. Fifth Mesa Holy People do as they please. You know that." He stared at her as he rubbed his cup. "I'm positive that he and my mother only wanted them to be safe."

"Damn!" May shouted, "I'm tired of them meddling in our affairs." Trying to remain calm, she drank from the cup—allowing the tea to take its own journey without interruption. She remembered how much value Coyote and Ava used placed on the ceremony— reaching into the consciousness of what the Japanese called Sabi. She waited until Coyote put down his cup. "I'm positive that they also had something to do with blowing up the moon."

Coyote slowly shook his head, "I know nothing about that."

May carefully watched his eyes. When he looked up she smiled. "Our survival of the Third Mesa depends on those children."

Coyote glanced at the cedar tree that was growing in the garden. He tried to think of its Japanese name but it was gone from his memory. He shook his head. "General Liberty," he said quietly, "our only hope is for you to stop this war."

May banged down her cup. "I can't stop this war, and you, of all people, should realize that."

"If you stop killing the men," he answered, "perhaps some of

42

your women just might start having children again." He clapped his hands together. "It's really a very simple concept."

May stood up and walked over to the one window in the room. "I could have you shot for such talk."

"I'm sure you could."

"You don't seem frightened."

"Perhaps it would be a blessing."

May walked back to the table. "Try and remember, Coyote, that it was not the women who started the first war." She put her hands on her hips and challenged him with her stance. "Back in the mid-eighties all of our tax money was being spent on the military. For those phallic missiles that had their own code of male terminology—deep penetration, terminal thrust, hard and soft targets. And you males, my dear friend, blew this world apart with your weapons, and then, like typical male lovers, despised it for its submission."

Coyote remained seated. He finished the tea and rubbed the rim of the cup which symbolized purification. It was true, he thought to himself, the males had been out of control, and there was nothing left for the women but to fight for survival. That was when May, with her army, took over Wandering Foot. Ava joined them and he was forced into the desert. "I think it's all too late," he said.

May stared in silence. The guns had started up again. "Are you aware that the men's army is only a few miles from the rim?"

"I know that," Coyote answered, "I stole one of their trucks."

"So you must realize that they want this canyon, the women, and the water because there is nothing left out there." She sat down and Coyote could see how tired she looked. "And, as you also know, because you fought with the men for so many years, that once we surrender . . ." She couldn't finish the sentence. "Right?"

Coyote was thinking about all of the killing, the raping, the trophies of breasts, labias, scalps. The men were counting on an unconditional surrender. They had regressed that far. Submission or extinction. Nothing could stop them. Now, their only reason for fighting was perversion. Coyote turned back. His eyes told her the answer. He ran his fingers through his long blue-black hair. "Right . . ."

"So we fight on."

Coyote studied the two guards outside the shoji. "I refuse to fight anymore." He stood up and walked across the tatami mats, paused at the entrance to the reception room and turned. "Do as you please with me."

May followed Coyote through the doors. "For your own safety I must keep you under house arrest," she said, as she motioned for the guards to intercept her advisory. "For right now, being alive is much more important to us than being dead." She looked at her watch. "We'll be having a late dinner. My advisors, Molly if you'd like . . . say around ten."

Coyote opened the fusumas. "I do not plan to go anywhere." He stepped onto the veranda. The fragrance of the camelia blossoms greeted his saddened spirit. A school of koi swam in a pond below the veranda. He bent down as they flashed beneath the water lilies. When he saw May's reflection in the water he stood up. "Perhaps you could have some sake sent to my room." He felt a fine spray of water blow across his face as a miniature rainbow arched over the split-log bridge.

May brushed away a mosquito that had settled on her forehead. "You will try to locate your brother?"

Coyote laughed, and he didn't know why. Perhaps, he thought to himself, because he really didn't have the power anymore to do that. All he could do was hope for the best. The Fifth Mesa seemed centuries away, and he didn't even know how to think about his former home. "Sure, why not, and I'll see if I can pick up a used moon somewhere."

May, who had walked over to the edge of the veranda quickly spun around. "Your brother probably had something to do with blowing up the moon," she said, as she moved toward Coyote like she was stalking him. "He thinks he's such a hot shot with that trombone of his. His musical prick . . . that's all it is."

Quietly, as if an old, shy memory tried to slip unnoticed into Coyote's consciousness, he picked up a vague feeling of a plan to recreate extinct species with Kid and Dali–Kibbutz. Kid was standing on a rock in the middle of a flowered meadow like a musical conductor, and he was buried in the tall grasses and wild flowers with Dali. Kid was waving his trombone and hundreds of bubbles were floating around in the sky. Coyote sighed. Everyday was a holiday when they were together. They only managed to bring back the Tasmanian owl and a couple of others that he had forgotten. A pigeon or something like that. He smiled and looked over at the general. "You know," he said as he suddenly had the feeling that his brother was close by, "Kid would have never made it down here on the Third Mesa, May. You know that as well as I do. He's much too kind."

"Sweet my ass." May motioned for her guards to assist Coyote to the guest cottage. "I will see you at ten, Tuesday Coyote."

As the two guards approached Coyote, the dragontail landed on his head, and then quickly flew off. He watched it fly over the lake. He looked back at May and laughed. "That was my brother telling me that you're a real hard-ass." He touched his finger to his forehead. "See you at ten."

Kid, crouched behind a Japanese red pine, had been surveying the nighttime activities of Wandering Foot for over an hour. Between the movements of the supply trucks, the outer perimeter guards, and the soldiers who were placed around the women's quarters, he had been able to slip through the grounds and find his brother and Molly having supper with May and her staff. He had decided, since he was extremely anxious to see his brother, that the front door was the best way to make his move. It would also eliminate a lot of sneaking around. However, he would have to face General Liberty, and he had no idea what she would do to him. But, if Tuesday could do it, so could he.

He also had been trying to come up with a scheme that would truly impress Coyote, nudge Molly along the lovesick trail, and hopefully, give Ms Liberty a giant-sized kick in the pants of her heavily starched military uniform. He also wanted to show his brother just how much he had improved since their last performance together. His brother had been such a natural at everything, and he used to give Kid such a hard time for being so crude. However, that was a long time ago, and he felt like he had finally mastered his craft since their last medicine show.

When Kid finally hit on his plan of attack, he reached down into his pack and pulled out a beaded bottle that had been Chief Joseph's dream collector. It was full of Kid's wizard potion, or what his father had always called his Trickster-of-Elixir. He shook the bottle, passed it randomly over his head to gather in all of the six directions, mumbled out an old ragged prayer to anyone who cared or dared listen, and emptied the contents into the bell of his rose-gold pawnshop trombone.

"Come on shoo-fly," he coaxed, as he rubbed the bell and checked the slide, "we've got to give old snake oil Coyote something that will raise the fur on his spine to a shivering religiosamente, revive the Battle of Little Bighorn on the back of his neck, make his dandruff turn into snow leopards. Just a subtle extravaganza that will let Iron Pants Liberty know that Kid Monday is back in town. And to that beautiful Tibetan-Apache rose petal, just a sweet kiss on the left breast."

He stepped out from behind the pine, tested the wind with a moistened finger, wiped his silver-tipped imagination on the back of his strange and sometimes perverted fantasy and aimed his trombone into the moonless sky. With a maestro's concern for perfection, he ran through his entire performance, and when he felt that he had it exactly perfect, he gently touched his lips to the mouthpiece and blew out the bubble. It came out perfectly round, the size of a normal seven and five-eights fool's halo. As it floated over the villa, it began to expand, and when it reached its full maturity, it jiggled, gave out a few puffs of colored smoke, and then exploded into a brilliant shower of colored lights. There were rainbows tucked inside paper swans, sunrises in the yin and the yang of sunsets, whales spinning counterclockwise around the outside of an enormous mandala. And inside the center of this pulsating circle was The Mother Goddess who was looking extremely voluptuous, Fifth Mesa sensitive and third Mesa tough. There was an aura of yonis and lingums moving around her head—laced together by spring flowers, vas deferens, and fallopian tubes.

The guards tried to shoot it down but Kid's overture was impervious to outside intervention. When they finally realized that they were not being invaded they dropped on their knees to witness The Mother smiling like a pat of butter inside a steaming winged

48

potato as she flew across the sky.

Molly raced to the sliding panels, opened the inner screen and stepped out onto the veranda to see The Mother pull on a pair of leather racing gloves and climb into the cab of a baked enamel maroon and black Peterbilt tractor. She looked back at Coyote and May who were seated on the tatami mats.

"Coyote," she yelled, "it's the Mother Goddess." As she turned around, she heard the blasting of air horns, the down shifting of gears, and then she saw the tractor sail across the sky, execute the Tibetan Knot of Eternity, leave a wake of stars and rainbows, knock out a string of fleurs-de-lis just so the followers of Occidental Thought wouldn't get their noses bent out of shape and then head for the front door. All of the tractor's lights were flashing, tires were screeching, brakes smoking and the tape deck was blasting out a women's revolutionary fight song. Molly raised her fist and then followed everyone against one wall. Everyone, that is, except Coyote, who remained on the mat. He took out a Turkish cigarette, tapped the end on his fingernail and casually lighted it just as Kid's ordained truck came flying through the building.

Coyote took a long, deep drag and put the smoke into the middle of the room in tight, neat circles. The Peterbilt slowly dissolved inside the curling of Coyote's smoke ring. When Kid's catastrophe vanished on the edge of his brother's nose, Molly, May, and her advisors cautiously walked to the front of the room to see Kid Monday materialize as if created from Coyote's imagination. He wore a tweed sport coat, faded jeans, a silver buckle with the Mother Goddess and the Cowboy Buddha shaking hands on home plate at the 1987 World Series, and a baseball cap that read, "Beware of the Wizard." His infamous trombone was in one hand, pack over one shoulder, and in his other hand he held a bunch of wild flowers brought down from the Fifth Mesa. He handed the flowers to Molly, gave General Liberty his very best sunday punch smile and sat down next to his brother. "Tues," he said, as he put his arm around Coyote's neck, "you old smoke-belching cayuse, I'm reporting for duty."

Coyote raised his sun glasses and looked at Kid with playful contempt. "Kid, you have a calling card as sloppy as an elephant waltzing in a bucket of lumpy mush. You'd think that after all of those informative years of riding with the Coyote you'd stop calling out these insensitive pranks. Tacky . . . just low class tacky."

Coyote stood up and walked around Kid as if he were inspecting his brother. "I kept telling you about subtlety and understatement." He shook his head and winked.

May seemed to be in shock, but Kid didn't care. "Madame Liberty," he said, as he pointed to his brother, "has this ol' diesel Sasquatch been giving you as much crap as he always gave me?"

May stepped closer to Kid and put her hands on her narrow hips. "Kid Monday, I and my staff were not amused by your insipid, tasteless entrance, and I can assure you that unless you decide to bring back our children, you and your brother will not leave Wandering Foot alive." She walked around him as she popped a swagger stick against the palm of her hand.

Kid only laughed. He took off his hat, scratched his blond head and slapped the cap back on. He knew, from talking to Molly, that May could be mean, but he was hoping to keep her pacified in order to figure out how to get his brother and Molly out of Wandering Foot. On his way down from Mesa-Five he had seen the battle that was being fought on both rims. It would be only a matter of days before the men broke through. "Well, the reason I came down here," he said in a soft drawl, "is to tell you that we've decided to let you and your soldiers onto the Fifth Mesa." He slowly began to disassemble his trombone. "Besides, the kids are just too much trouble for the old farts up there. A big pain in their tepidamente butts, if you get my drift."

"What?" May yelled. "You're asking us to come up and be the baby sitters for our children?"

Kid looked over at Molly and winced. "Well, it would sure beat being annihilated."

"Kid Monday . . . you're a bigger fool than I thought," May replied.

Kid stepped closer to his brother. "You look like hell," he said under his breath.

"You should have seen me a week ago," Coyote answered.

"Can you finagle a way to get us alone for awhile?"

Coyote nodded.

May stared at Kid. "If you don't have those children back here by noon tomorrow I'll see to it that you and your brother are sent to the front." She pointed at finger at him. "No tricks."

Kid shrugged and looked sheepishly over at Coyote. "You and me as cannon fodder. Could be worse."

Molly cut in front of Kid and confronted May, "Why don't you let them be alone in the hot pools for awhile. I'm sure the water would be good for them."

May, tapping her swagger stick, stepped over to Coyote. "Since we talked last, Coyote, I think we just might have a bead on your wife." She rested the stick against Coyote's chest. "Therefore I suggest that you and your arrogant brother behave yourselves." She looked over at Kid's trombone that was on one of the back tables. "We'll keep this, Kid Monday, just in case you get any strange ideas about busting out of here."

Kid bowed, and nudged Coyote.

May ordered two of the guards to escort the two brothers to the hot springs.

"Sweet woman," Kid said, as they were leaving the building. Coyote was in front of him. Molly, not wanting to jeopardize her position with the General, remained.

Coyote noticed that May was behind them. "I'm certain that we can figure something out right away." He stepped into the reception room. "And maybe, if it wouldn't be too much trouble, perhaps you could have some sake sent over."

Kid turned and faced May. "It was a great pleasure to visit your queendom . . ."

Coyote grabbed Kid by the coat and pulled him out the door. "Cut the crap."

Kid proceeded to back out the door. "I take it, General Maybelle, that I'm being held in protective custody . . . somewhat . . . how would I say, like . . . ah . . . sotovoce."

May raised her head and a gleam snapped into her eyes. She followed him through the door. "Definitely, Maestro Monday, but let's just say that it's more . . . how would you say it up there on your podium . . . maybe sostenuto." She clapped her hands together. "Yes, that's exactly it."

April Fools and Spider Woman were escorting the children back from the Seventh Mesa's Hall of Fame. They stopped at the mesa's edge where they could look down on the Third Mesa. Firefights were on both rims and every few minutes a flare would explode and float into the canyon. Blocked by the walls, the explosions were gruff warnings that the battle was being pushed into Wandering Foot.

The Children stood transfixed as they watched the tracer bullets, mortar shells, and flares crisscrossing the southern hemisphere. Although it was after ten in the evening, everyone's features were visible. A warm wind was blowing off the desert. April Fools grabbed Michi's hand to keep him from stepping too close to the edge. "What a contrast," he said, as he picked up the boy.

"From the Seventh Mesa to this," Spider Woman added.

"It's like watching a video game made in a foreign noise," LaMar said. "It doesn't seem real."

"To me," Rosie added, "it's like having a part of your body destroyed by an incurable disease."

Spider Woman leaned against a large rock.

"As long as I can remember we've tried to help, but they wouldn't listen to us."

"Give us more weapons," April Fools said in a distorted voice that resembled a gravel-throated robot. "We want to kill . . ."

"Why don't you make them Holy People?" Heidi asked, as she sat down next to Spider Woman. "That's what I would do."

"Oh yeah," the smallest girl countered, "then they would make war up here."

"And keep on hurting everyone like they're doing down there," Michi added.

"We can't," Spider Woman answered, as she took Heidi's hand and placed it over her heart. "It's from here." She touched Heidi's head. "And here. It must be earned, but still, each mesa is invaluable to each other."

"How could the Third Mesa be valuable to anything?" Jamal asked.

Spider Woman picked up a large rock. "You see," she said, as she took a black felt marker and quickly divided up the rock into sections, "the planet is like a large brain. Every part is dependent upon each other, and so it's extremely important that everything works well together." She pointed to where the Parietal lobe would be. "Here is the Seventh Mesa." She tapped the top of the rock. "Now, over here in the Occipital lobe is the Fifth Mesa, and near the Frontal lobe is the Fourth Mesa, and your former home is down here at the Temporal lobe. Without every section working, we can't have a whole planet."

"And when it rains that's called a brain storm," Jamal said, as he punched LaMar in the arm.

"Get out of here," April Fools yelled.

"Why are some mesas more highly developed than others?" Rosie asked.

A long series of explosions lighted up the entire rim of the Fifth Mesa. Spider Woman looked over at April Fools. A sad smile rose within her. "It's all the things you heard about on the Seventh Mesa, kids. Peace, beauty, harmony . . ."

"It's what makes things grow . . . right?"

"And lots of hard work," April Fools added.

"Yuk, I hate hard work," Jamal said.

"Ahhhh . . . but it can be fun," Spider Woman replied to Jamal, "like when we return to the Seventh Mesa to explore new routes to some of the higher mesas."

"When I grow up I'm going to live on the Seventh Mesa with Pollen Boy and Buddha Shooting Way," Michi said.

"I think we should zap the Third Mesa with a big sleep gun," LaMar said proudly.

"Yo," Spider Woman said as she stood up. "That's what we tried to do and ended up blowing up the moon." She started down the trail. "We've never been very good at influencing other mesas with our experiments."

"The Great Mother did that, didn't she?" Rosie asked.

"Mona . . ."

"She's weird . . ."

"Shhhh . . . !" Spider Woman said dramatically, "She feels very bad about that."

"I like her," the youngest girl said, "besides, she's Kid's mother."

April Fools started walking on his hands. "I like her because she lets me win in the one-armed hand race."

"You're silly."

Jamal stood on his hands and started down the trail. "See, this is the way to really develop your brain." He took ten steps. "Peace through gravity's underwear."

"Bikini peace," April Fools added. "That's for me."

"How about laughs?" LaMar asked.

"How about tickles?" Heidi shouted, as she began to tickle April Fools.

"Hey . . . knock it off."

Spider Woman took Rosie's and Scotty's hands as they followed the faster children down the trail. She was amazed at how quickly they were responding to the Holy People, and the Hall of Famers gave them so much hope and desire to go on. "Soon," she thought to herself, "they'll be pushing beyond the Seventh Mesa, and then who knows where they'll go." She smiled and squeezed the childrens' hands. "I can hardly wait . . ."

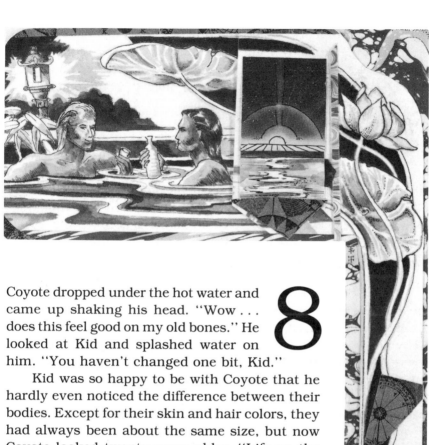

Coyote dropped under the hot water and came up shaking his head. "Wow . . . does this feel good on my old bones." He looked at Kid and splashed water on him. "You haven't changed one bit, Kid."

8

Kid was so happy to be with Coyote that he hardly even noticed the difference between their bodies. Except for their skin and hair colors, they had always been about the same size, but now Coyote looked twenty years older. "Life on the fabled land of Mesa-Five, Tues, you know what it's like."

Coyote shook his head. "Peaceful," he answered, as he glanced over at Kid as if to challenge him. He rubbed the long scar on his right shoulder where a bayonet had pinned him to a willow tree. "It's the land of enlightened whackos all geritoled-out for the mega-millenium humping from one higher consciousness to another in your vacuum packaged Dreamstreamers." He dipped down so that his shoulders were covered. "Now that's what I call divine intervention."

Kid laughed as he walked along the sandy bottom toward Coyote. "And you, cruise control that you are, haven't changed one bit. He splashed Coyote with water. "I'm amazed that we are so different."

"It's archetypically accurate, ol' buddy," Coyote replied, as he reached over to a large rock in the middle of the pool where Kid had put the tray of hot sake and cups. He filled two cups and handed one to Kid. "It's so easy that it's boring." He smiled and raised his glass. "No offense Mon, but we chose to ride the polarities and . . ."

"You'd never be happy back home?" Kid interrupted.

"Come on Kid," Coyote replied, as he finished his sake. "Drink up." He put his cup on the tray and drank from the jug. "There's about enough sake here for two midget mosquitoes." He looked over at the guard. "Tell the cook to send out five gallons," he shouted, as he rubbed his chest. He sighed and then laughed. "Ahhh . . . hot sake, Mon . . . it's like being fucked by a toothless hummingbird."

Kid, who had just taken a sip of sake, blew it over Coyote. "Shit," he shouted.

Coyote cocked his head as he watched a flare slowly fall into the lake by the main villa. "It's beautiful, isn't it." He smiled, but it was only for himself. "Death is so much more challenging than life, y'know, Mon. It's like great poetry that has distilled life right down to one breath." He looked over at his brother. "It just cuts out all of the crap." He watched another flare. "I've never had to call bullshit on a dying person. It just gets fucking real." A guard stepped across the rocks and put a new tray of sake on the bank. Coyote flipped a finger to his forehead. "Thanks amiga . . ." He filled another cup for his brother and floated it over to him on the tray. "So, Mom's shed the heavy burden of motherhood, and gone aerobic." He sipped from the sake bottle. "I think, Kid, perhaps sake is more like getting blown by your favorite poem. How much intimate can you get." He raised the jug. "So . . . you think Ava's right here at Wandering Foot?"

"That's what the kids told me, Tues."

"You mean to tell me that General Maytag lied to me?"

Kid laughed. He had forgotten how happy Coyote could be when he was drunk. However, he did remember that there was a point when he would suddenly get meaner than broken glass. He swam over to a moss covered rock. "How beautiful this night is with the brushing of bamboo against the stones, the subtle fragrance of jasmine that's just about to bloom, the slapping of the water. All we need is a full moon, Molly and Ava with us, and . . . ," he looked over at his brother, "and peace."

Coyote was silent as he watched the flares' and lanterns' reflection in the water. "I can see the moon's reflection in the water, Kid . . . so it must be up there someplace." He slowly walked into the center of the pool. "I always wanted to fuck the moon, Kid." He quickly looked over at his brother. "Y'know . . . it was so fucking sensual floating up there and all it did was give me an erection. That big floating sphere of woman. . ." He slowly began to rub his breasts. "And that brilliant madman, The Whoa . . . Man, and our beloved mother . . . Mona." He laughed and winked at Kid. "That's what you said, right? Mona . . . ?" He shook his head. "It's one of the best jokes of all times, Kid, Atomic and laser energy saddled up together on a wild ride through the peace movement on a passive bull market." Again, he laughed. "I can't believe it." He put the sake bottle on the floating tray and ducked under the water. When he surfaced he reached for the jug and took a long drink. "That's what is called in my coyote dictionary . . . Coyote Dumb." He rubbed his head, and pulled the braid out of his hair. "I really should be looking for my wife."

Kid lifted himself onto a rock. "I'll find her for you," he said, as he looked around the pool. He counted seven guards.

"Is that why you came down here?" Coyote asked.

Kid paused, as he tried to sort out what Tuesday meant. "Naw . . . I needed a vacation," he answered, as he kicked water onto Coyote.

"Yeah, and so do the angels." Coyote walked toward his brother. "You came down here to save my ass, right?" He grabbed Kid's foot. "And, to slip your magic marker into Molly, grab Ava as you swing through the bamboo, and maybe, if the script is just right, save the day." He raised his hands into the air. "Touchdown!"

"Get out of here."

"Ha, I'm right."

"Come on, Tues, I just wanted to see you."

"You are a sentimental shit." He grabbed Kid's feet and pulled him off the rock. Kid grabbed onto Coyote's neck and pushed him under the water. They scrambled and playfully fought with each other. Only after a few minutes of grabass did Kid realize that Coyote was trying to hurt him. He also realized that his brother didn't have the strength he used to have. Kid pushed Coyote away and stepped back. "Okay, you win . . ." Kid swam over to a deep hole and dived under the water. It made him extremely sad to think that Coyote was so angry, but there was nothing he could do, or even say. When he emerged, he saw that Coyote had started on the third bottle of sake. He climbed out of the pool and sat down on a wooden bench. He reached over and touched the trunk of a flowering plum. Coyote slowly stepped out of the water and sat down next to Kid.

"I'm sorry about that, Kid . . . I guess I got kinda carried away."

Kid touched Coyote's knee and looked at his brother. "That's all right, Tues. You know, you always used to win our fights, but I think I was so intimidated by you that I would just let you win." He rubbed his neck. "You were always so serious."

"Ha . . . you've found out my secret." He poured a cup of sake and handed it to Kid. "It's good to see you . . . brother."

Kid looked into Coyote's eyes. "Thanks."

There was a series of loud explosions on the north rim. Kid jumped, but Coyote looked around as if he didn't hear the noise. "When I was out there in the desert, I would dream about the two of us together again so we could put our skills together to do something really great." He pointed to the south rim. "Like stop the war."

Kid laughed and put his arm around Coyote's shoulders. "Maybe we could create another moon, Tues."

Coyote shook his head and looked down at his feet. "I don't think I've got it anymore."

"Ahh . . . come on."

"No . . . it's true." He looked at the sake cup and picked up the jug. "There's nothing in here anymore. Just blank pages of mildewed paper." He chortled and rubbed Kid's hair with his knuckles.

"Hey!" Kid shouted, as he jumped up.

Coyote walked over to another bench and picked up a towel. He started to wipe his genitals. He grabbed his penis. "Look at this limp noodle," he said.

"Whoa there . . . you're going to rip if off."

"It wouldn't matter, hoss . . . it hasn't worked in years."

Kid walked over to the alcove where Coyote was standing. Coyote threw him a towel. "A war wound . . . ?"

"No, it just got lost in translation somewhere," Coyote answered. "I guess it got bored with me being angry, pissed off, drunk with opium stuck up my butt so it just flew away." Coyote laughed, and looked at Kid's penis. "You probably have it, Mon." He got down on his knees and stared at his brother's cock. "Yes, this is it. I can tell because it's so much better looking than that little needle-dick

60

you used to have." He grabbed Kid's penis and looked at its head. "Ah ha . . . of course . . . it says Made for Coyote Silk." Coyote looked up at his brother. "I want this back."

Kid jumped away and flipped Coyote's ass with his towel. "Keep away from my tallywhacker! I won this at the fair by lobbing Cherrios around a hummingbird's pecker. It speaks two hundred languages, it can be used to store water when traveling across deserts, and, when needed, dear brother, we can use it as a telephone to call up Mona." He grabbed his penis and pulled it as far as it would stretch. "Hi mom."

Coyote sat down on the bench and wrapped a towel around his neck. "Someday, we're both going to be reincarnated as skidrow pawnshops." He laughed and lowered his head. "Where's the booze?" He emptied the jug and looked up at Kid. "Sorry about that."

Kid joined Coyote. "Y'know Tues, you're just about the most handsome man I've ever seen in my entire life." He looked over at Coyote and studied his face. "You're a little beat up, you've got a bum leg that makes you walk like Marco Polio, your dick don't work, but other than that . . . you're a perfect specimen of incipient assholery."

"Thanks Kid," Coyote answered, as he wrapped up his head in his towel. "And just who is more handsome than I?"

"Me of course."

"Naturally." Coyote slapped Kid's leg, put his towel at the end of the bench and laid down with his feet on his brother's lap. "Y'know Kid, earlier, at the villa, you could have impressed May a lot more by floating a Bashō haiku through the front door on a basket of bamboo flowers."

Kid looked at Coyote's feet. "I know," he answered. "I guess I blew it."

Coyote laughed as he lifted up his head. "Would you run to the store and get me some drugs?"

"Sure . . . what flavor?"

"It don't matter, hoss, as long as it's down and dirty." He pulled his kimono over his body and looked at the stars. "Fuck, am I beat."

Kid shook the sake jug. "Thanks for saving me some."

"Sure, don't mention it." He took another dry towel and folded it over his face. "Wake me up in an hour or so, Mon, I'm just goin' to take a little snooze." He lifted off the towel, "And while I'm communicating with the devil you should be figuring out how to get us out of this shithole, find Ava, save Molly . . . which should be easy for someone like yourself because you're older than I, you've got the only dick that works, or I assume it does since it's really mine, plus . . . you are under my command because I am . . . the Coyote."

A series of huge explosions ripped the silence beyond the upper lakes. "Whoa," Kid exclaimed, as he jumped from the noise, "I can't believe that we're down here when everything is caving in." He looked up at the canyon wall when he heard another explosion. A red flare floated off the rim. The guards didn't seem to be paying much attention to the battle being fought on both sides of the canyon. "Yeah, go to sleep, Tues, I'll find a way to get us out of here."

Coyote didn't answer. Kid leaned over and looked into his face. He had fallen asleep. "But first," he said to himself, "I need some breathing room." Kid slipped Coyote's feet onto the bench and walked over to the hot pool. Despite everything, he mused, it was a beautiful spring night. The guards were still in their same places, and two more had been stationed above the pool. "I guess they're probably happier here than up on the front," he said quietly, "and perhaps I can provide them with some entertainment." He walked around the semi-cultivated garden until he found what he was looking for. He took a small knife from his kimono pocket, cut down a piece of bamboo, and carefully began to make a Shakuhachi. He knew how much Coyote used to enjoy flute music, and perhaps it would be a way to come up with a plan. If he couldn't perform his magic, at least he could make music. The piece he cut was exactly twenty-two inches. After he had put in the four top holes and one in back, he began to meticulously fashion the oblique blowing edge. When he felt that he had it as perfect as it could be, he polished the inside with the end of Coyote's kimono wrapped around a smaller piece of bamboo. He tested the instrument and found it to have a soft, reedy tone—exactly the way a Shakuhachi should sound. He ran through the scales, emphasizing the half steps common to traditional Japanese. He fine-tuned the mouthpiece and then returned to the bench. Coyote was still asleep. Perhaps, Kid thought, he could serenade his brother into a new body, or a vision to create another moon.

Sitting cross-legged on a tatami mat, he began to play a simple melody that came easily through his body—like the wind blowing through him—he only transcribed what was already there. His desire was to make it serene and beautiful—a translation of emptiness.

Losing track of time, he became aware of the budding jasmine trees, the almost bashful fragrance they were offering him. It wasn't exactly their time to blossom, but their nubile succulence promised to be delicious. He allowed the aroma to enter his body as he interpreted the scent and passed it through the flute to everything around him. The music was a capturing of the flower, freeing it into another form—expressing its deep beauty and how it made him feel after being away for so long.

Lost inside the inner garden, he played until he no longer had any thoughts of himself, forgetting where he was and why he was there. If peace were possible, he slowly began to realize, it could only come from such simple acts as playing the flute or bathing in pools.

The guards, who couldn't help but listen to the music, became aware of a stronger aroma than they were accustomed to in the garden. And for some strange reason, they felt as if the jasmine's blossoms were overpowering their bodies. Slowly, they put down their weapons and settled themselves comfortably on the bench.

Kid heard the chimes from the bronze bell that signaled midnight. He had been playing for over two hours. The air had cooled, and a tickling breeze was blowing down the canyon. He felt emptied of any illusions about what he wanted to do. He was happy, and from that came a purity from letting go. When he started to play once again, the music was the pure sound of the jasmine, and then . . . as if someone had blinked, he was gone. Kid had changed himself into the Kuchinashi—the scent of the Cape Jasmine.

What disturbed Ava Matisse more than being May's prisoner was that she had been locked up in the hideout that she had built for herself years ago. Set in a **9** high cut above Wandering Foot, the structure was a masterpiece of architecture and discipline. It was her haven among the clouds, and designed to synthesize her inner feeling into a place where the subconscious would travel.

It had been her nest; having it used as a jail was the worst insult she could imagine, and May knew that.

The hike up was long, arduous, and designed to pass through climatic and geological zones, until she reached her own private Aerie. Sometimes she would only remain there for a few hours, a day, two, and other times for weeks.

Looking up from the canyon floor, Ava had always marveled at its remoteness, and how she had been able to build it. But upon arrival, when looking back at Wandering Foot, she had the same feelings about the place she had left. So simple in design, only inspiration could possibly follow.

Ava was also surprised that May had never

used the Aerie, and could only think of it as a place of punishment. Secluded, it had to be a part of the General's plan.

Ava could also tell by watching the guards that something was happening below. Being so close to the rim, they seemed extremely nervous. All night long the fighting had been going on. They must be scared and confused, she thought, but she didn't know how she could help them. She also knew that she could escape, but where could she go? And would she want to flee by herself? If only she knew Coyote's whereabouts they could take off for the Fifth Mesa. But May had told her that her husband had been killed. She didn't feel it was true, but even then, how could she find out? All she could do was keep the faith. Coyote was out there, someplace.

Ava walked out onto the cantilevered veranda. Across the canyon she could see the gun battles and watch the continual barrage of flares. It all seemed like a movie to her. Somewhere or somehow, her emotions had died out there in the battlefields. Her survival instincts told her that she could survive, but she didn't know why. For what?

It seemed that all of the Holy Highs had finally given up on everyone.

The wind was blowing and she felt a wisp of water from the falls that dropped over the trail. Along with it came a breath of spring flowers, but it was too early for the Aerie's vegetation to be in bloom. It had to be the scent from her favorite plant. Yes, she could occasionally catch its odor.

*   *   *   *   *

As Molly walked around her small garden, she couldn't stay away from the reflecting pool. She was so overwhelmed by her inner feelings that she needed to share them with someone.

Hugging herself, she sat down on the stone bench. After she had left the main villa, she retired to the small house that she had lived in since her arrival in Wandering Foot. The garden had been built in the same classical manner as all of the gardens in the canyon: by understatement—the beauty within nature reduced to a minimum of representation. In the center of her dry garden was a large moss covered rock that was to her another mesa—a place of peace and harmony—surrounded by the perfectly raked sand. During the time she had been involved in the war, it was her only inner world of beauty.

66

As she sat by the reflecting pool she wished for two things. Peace, she realized, would probably never happen, at least in her lifetime. Her second dream, which seemed as impossible as having peace, was for the moon. It seemed such a simple request. She had hung a paper lantern from a tree so that when she looked into the pool, its reflection resembled the moon. She only had to close her eyes and there it was, exactly as she remembered, except that she couldn't feel it inside her body. There was a deep emptiness, and nothing could fill it, not even the end of the war.

As she began thinking wistfully about Kid, the same sensation kept calling her to the pool. She wanted to see how she looked when he was watching her, or how she smiled when he would flirt with her. Only with Kid had she experienced those feelings, and they ran through her like ancient shivers. In fact, they felt so good that eventually she didn't want to think about anything else.

She could smell the jasmine and it was so much stronger than before. In fact, she mused, it felt as if the aroma was caressing her skin. She rubbed her arms, walked to the edge of the garden and stood underneath a drooping cherry tree. How strange, she thought, that Wandering Foot could be invaded at any moment, and all she could think about was seeing Kid. But soon, she would have to return to the hospital for another twenty-four hour shift. She should rest, but there was no hope. She knew she had to wait. She thought she could see his face, but upon examination it was only the kasuga-dora lighting the path. She closed her eyes and said a quiet prayer.

*   *   *   *   *

Kid, passing through the exterior gardens, laughed as the guards spoke about the amazing fragrance that had crossed the path.

"The wind is blowing down the canyon," one guard said, as she looked around the garden. "The jasmine is so much stronger than I can ever remember."

"It must be the wet spring we had."

"Or the war . . ."

"The last chance to bloom."

"That's too fucking morbid, Sarah."

"I can't help it, I'm scared."

"Honey, we all are, but at least we're down here and not up on the rim. I hear that we're holding our own."

"Yes, for how long?"

"Until the men run out of food, water, and ammo."

"And then what?"

"Peace," one of them shouted, "what else would you want?"

Sarah stood up and walked in a circle. "Did you know that Molly bribed the guard who was keeping Kid Monday's trombone?"

"What can she do with it?"

"I wonder what General May is going to do with Kid and Coyote."

"Or with Ava Matisse."

"At least she's up at the Aerie and out of the way. If they do break through they won't find her for days."

"Who knows?"

"I'm so tired," Sarah said, "I think I'll walk around the hot pools."

Kid twisted himself around their faces to thank them for their information, flew beyond the women's quarters, past the aviary, slipped through the branches of a Blue Japanese oak and looked over Molly's bamboo wall. He could see Molly's reflection inside the paper moon that was being cast in the water. It was almost a perfect eclipse. He wished, for only a second, that he had the audacity to change himself into a real moon, but he shook it off as an insensitive tease. He dropped down Molly's head, as he mixed up his scent with all the other flowers in the garden.

Molly lifted her head and looked around. "Oh . . . ," she gasped, and took a deep breath. The aroma was so intense that she almost fell off the bench. She caught herself, and when she turned back, Kid's image was floating inside her reflection.

"Kid?" she questioned.

He put a finger over his lips. "Careful, the guards will be looking for me."

"How did you get here?"

Kid pulled out the flute. "I had to see you."

Molly looked suspiciously around the garden. "I didn't hear the gate open."

Kid's laughter gave him away.

"Ahhhh . . . ," she responded to his grin. She took the flute and lovingly caressed it with her fingertips.

Kid's smile broadened. He shrugged. "Since my trombone was confiscated, I had to come up with something." Molly returned the flute. He played a few notes. "Not too much horsepower, but it got me here." He looked through the sodegaki to see if he had been

68

followed.

"Where's your brother?" she asked.

"Sleeping at the hot springs."

"Is he okay?"

"He's a little drunk." Kid watched Molly's face as if it were a delicate flower. "He'll be safe until we can come up with a plan." He laughed, and flipped the flute into the air. "I don't think this little kingyo has the pizzazz to get us out of here."

Molly, wanting to keep Kid as long as possible, didn't tell him that she had Cheyenne Rose. She started to feel guilty, but quickly brushed it off. Perhaps she reasoned to herself, it would make him more like an ordinary person. She smiled. "You must have brought the jasmine into blossom," she said, as she watched him flip the shakuhachi.

Kid caught it behind his back.

"I must admit, Kid," she said softly, that your entrance this time was a shade more delicate than before."

"Oh, you mean the Wagnerian Circus?"

Politely, Molly nodded her head, as a smile sauntered through her body. She couldn't believe that he was sitting so casually across from her when Wandering Foot could be invaded at any moment.

Kid, sensing her confusion, sat down on the grass and leaned his back against a Japanese black pine. "Ahhh . . . that's much better," he said as he felt the tree's thick bark. The pool was still between them and, with their reflections and the lantern's distorted image it made him feel that they were having a small garden party. He watched her in silence. Although he had known her since she was two, it was on her eighteenth birthday that he began to see Molly differently. For over a year he had been making up all kinds of excuses to visit the Third Mesa.

Molly noticed the truck lights coming down from the rim. Worried that they might be the enemy, she pointed toward the north wall.

Kid didn't bother to look. He leaned forward and continued to look at her face with complete admiration. "I love you, Molly," he said softly.

Molly heard the words as if a chime had gone off within her heart. It continued ringing until she could bear to look into his face. "You are amazing, Kid Monday," she said, as she kept the sound vibrating throughout her body.

"I am with you," he answered.

She looked around the inner garden as if she had to invite the whole setting into her heart. "Always." Three simultaneous explosions occurred by the upper falls where Coyote had left the stolen truck. Molly jumped. "I hate that noise." She walked over to a drooping cherry tree, grabbed a low branch and shook the tree. Hundreds of blossoms fell over her. Kid watched in fascination. He joined her. "I've got to get back to Coyote," he said.

"I know . . ."

"I overheard one of the guards say that Ava is being imprisoned at the Aerie."

"I knew it," Molly answered. "I knew she was alive." She touched Kid's cheek. "I just never saw her dead."

Kid touched her hand and she slowly wrapped his fingers inside her palm. "I'm going to try and get Coyote up there." He put his free arm around her shoulders. "And then I'll be back."

I'm supposed to meet with General Liberty in a few minutes."

"Stall her . . . please."

"I don't know, Kid," she answered, as she looked into his eyes. "I could try."

"We've got to get out of here before this place blows," Kid said, as he took her hands.

"Oh Kid . . ."

"Is there a place where I can meet you?"

"Kid, I'm concerned about the wounded."

"Molly," Kid pleaded, "if this fighting keeps up there isn't going to be any wounded." He shook the tree and a second cascade of blossoms fell over them. "May will not surrender and the men, despite the lack of water, can stay out there forever. Believe me."

"Kid, I don't know." She brushed a petal off his forehead. "Where could we go?"

A series of explosions went off by the water tanks. "I don't know, but I'll just bet the men are trying to knock out your water storage facilities."

Molly grabbed Kid and hugged him. "Okay . . . I'll meet you in an hour at Coyote's Shoin . . ."

"Where?" Kid asked. He felt someone behind him, and he quickly returned to his disguise. Molly watched him disappear. "Kid," she whispered, "please . . ." She turned around when she heard the gate open. May Liberty walked into her garden.

"Molly," May said, as she stopped near the black pine, "I was worried about you . . ."

Molly smelled the vanishing fragrance as it twirled around her head. She felt frightened, and she didn't know what to do. "Oh . . . okay," she replied.

May stepped onto the veranda and sat down on a tatami mat. She looked around the garden. "I have been informed that you bribed one of the guards for Kid's trombone."

Molly sat opposite May. "Yes."

"May I ask why?"

"Because I didn't want it destroyed." She looked up. "Kid's father and my stepfather were the best of friends at the old Cowboy Buddha Hotel, and I wanted to keep it as a memento." She shrugged, and smiled. "That's all."

May didn't answer as she studied Molly's eyes. Finally, the smallest of a smile cracked her posture. "I think I believe you, Molly Rose, because you've been such a wonderful nurse. But, I know that Kid has shown some interest in you, and so I think that I would feel better if you went up to the medic's station on the south rim."

Molly took a deep breath and closed her eyes. "When?" She looked up at the rim and realized that, despite the last series of explosions, the flares had stopped.

"I just received word that the men have pulled back." She sighed, and shook her head. "We'll be sending a convoy up there at 0600 hours. I want you to be on it."

"Where's Kid and Coyote?" Molly asked.

"They're asleep by the pool."

Molly furled her brow, but kept her head down. "Are they okay?"

"We have ten guards surrounding them, Molly, so please don't try anything heroic." She slowly walked down the stairs. "For sentimental reasons."

"May," Molly asked, as she followed her into the garden, "wouldn't it be better just to . . . ah . . . stop?"

May spun around and glared at the young woman. She stepped closer and pushed her swagger stick against Molly's breast. "I never want to hear those words again. Not from you or anyone else." She snapped the stick which grazed Molly's chin. "You got that?"

"Yes, General May," Molly replied.

"I hope so," May retorted. She spun around and stopped at the gate. "Just remember, there is no other place to go." May slapped the stick into her palm. "This is it."

Kid was determined to reunite his brother with Ava. After that, they would have to be on their own. He was becoming increasingly concerned about Molly and he realized that there wasn't much time left. Wandering Foot could be overrun at any moment.

10

He returned to his disguise and floated to the top of a Cryptomeria tree where he could get a fix on Coyote's guards.

A guard sniffed and looked at the tree. "The jasmine is back."

Kid felt like checking his armpits.

"Look, Coyote is awake."

"I heard that General Liberty is going to take them up to the front."

"I heard they'll be bringing Ava down from the Aerie."

Kid leaped into the air, took the flute and stuck it in the top branch where the wind would blow through the mouthpiece. After he had it securely in place, he dropped down next to his brother. Even before he could change back into his body, a fluttering one-pitched song began to sound. The guards jumped up and ran toward the noise.

"He's playing that damned flute again."

"It's our asses if May hears it."

"It's our dead asses because she'll send us up to the front."

"Honey, this is the front."

After they had run off, Kid returned to his body and sat next to Coyote. "Hey . . ."

Coyote looked over at his brother with tired, hung-over eyes. "Where have you been?"

"I'll tell you later." He helped Coyote up and took his hand. "I know where they're keeping Ava."

Coyote flipped a cigarette butt into the hot springs. "Where?"

"At the Aerie." Kid started pulling Coyote along the paved walk.

"Hey, go easy, hot shot," Coyote whispered, "my leg feels like it's filled with razor blades." Kid slowed down. They could hear the guards yelling about the music. "I was getting worried about you, Kid." They came to a stone bridge that crossed the river. Kid seemed confused as to which way to go. "Go that way," Coyote whispered, as he stopped to catch his breath.

Kid looked into Coyote's eyes. "You okay?"

"No . . ."

"Okay, then I'll carry you." He bent down and swooped Coyote over his shoulder.

"Hey," Coyote shouted.

"We don't have time to argue, Tues," Kid answered, "besides, I've just seen Molly and I'm full of love." He ran across the bridge and started up the trail. "How far is the Aerie's trailhead?"

"Thataway hoss, 'bout a few thousand miles," Coyote answered, in a gruff staccato voice.

"It'll be a breeze . . ."

"You're a masochist, Kid."

"That's what I keep hearing."

"Hey . . . I'm convinced."

Kid lumbered along the trail as he tried to stay away from the guards. Several times he ducked into the bushes when he heard them coming along the trail. After what seemed to be a long time of humping his brother, they came to a wooded area where he scooted behind three large boulders. Kid dropped Coyote onto the ground.

Coyote was rubbing his right knee. "I think you should donate

74

one of your legs to me. That way, we'd both have one good one."

Kid turned around and laughed. "Right or left?"

"It don't make nooo difference, hoss, they're both shot." Coyote limped over to a rock and sat down. "You are a strong mother." He looked up at the stars and took a deep breath. "Did you say Ava's at the Aerie?"

"That's what I heard, Tues."

Coyote looked up at the wall. "You can't see it from here, but it's a long ways up." Coyote felt in his pocket for his cigarettes. "You gonna carry me?"

Kid rubbed his shoulders. "One of the guards said that Ava was going to be brought down in the morning."

"That has an ominous sound to it . . ." Coyote held out the cigarette pack. "Want one?"

Kid pushed his hand away. "Are you nervous about seeing Ava?"

Coyote didn't answer until he had taken three drags from the cigarette. "That's one of the reasons I came in, Kid. To be with her again. All I care to remember were the good times we had together. I haven't been with a woman since."

Coyote's words felt like a knife into Kid's heart. "I know . . . you mentioned it back at the hot springs."

"It's true . . ."

"Why?" Kid asked into the darkness.

A quick burst of machine gun fire broke the silence. Kid and Coyote looked over to where it had come from. "A guard got spooked," Coyote said. He took a long drag and rubbed out the butt. "Why?" Coyote repeated, as he dug for the pack. "I never felt horny, Kid. Can you imagine that?" He struck another match inside his cupped hands. "There were lots of women. Camp followers, whores, even women who joined our side. But, it was a no go." He grabbed his crotch. "My heart just rode tough over my libido." He laughed, and looked over at Kid. "All I could think of was this incredibly beautiful woman." He paused and took a drag. "I was a fucking great warrior, Kid. I had no fear plus I was blessed with the ability to sense the enemy. Even the incoming fire. I just knew that there wasn't a bullet out there with my name on it." He touched Kid's arm. "But now, Kid . . . I think too much and feel nothing. Maybe Ava will make it different. I hope so." He slapped Kid's leg. "Now, all of the bullets have my name and I don't give a shit."

Kid sat in silence. He understood exactly what was going on with his brother. He could feel it, but he had nothing to say about it. Besides, he was certain that all of the words had been used up. Or, like Coyote said, there were no answers with his name on it. Kid touched Coyote's hand. "Molly said she would meet me at your old Shoin." He put out the unfinished cigarette. "What's that?"

"It's a little shack I built downriver as my own secret hideout. When Ava and I would blow up at each other she'd hightail it up to her spot, and I would go sulking thataway." He pointed down river. "It's where the river makes that big dogleg. Pooched out over the water in some big mother humpin' rocks." A smile slipped across Coyote's face like roadrunner with a bum leg. "Listen, the guns have stopped."

"I know."

Although he couldn't see his brother's face, Coyote looked at Kid as if he could. It felt good to him. He pulled Kid's wizard cap over his eyes. "Are you taking Molly out of here?"

"I hope she'll go with me." Kid took off the cap and put in on backwards. "She's torn about leaving Wandering Foot."

"Club her over the head and drag her out," Coyote suggested.

"Oh sure . . ." Kid laughed and looked over at his brother. "You have this gentle way about you."

"Ahhh . . . I was joking."

"Sure . . ."

Coyote glanced at both rims. "It's coming down tomorrow, Kid. I can feel it." He lighted another cigarette from the half-smoked one. He offered the pack to Kid.

Kid pushed it away.

"It's all right, Kid, Holy People live forever, or have you forgotten?"

"Not down here they don't."

"That's the best part," Coyote replied. He leaned over and tried to rub out the pain in his leg. "How did you sneak away from the hot springs?"

Kid laughed and wished that he had kept the shakuhachi. "Well," he said, as he followed a shooting star across the horizon, "I was able to make myself invisible for awhile."

"How?" Coyote asked, as he pointed toward the meteor. "Didn't General Maytag confiscate your trombone?"

"I don't need Cheyenne Rose no more, Tues. I've seen the

light." He jammed his elbow into Coyote's ribs. "You gonna have to hump yourself up that trail."

"Shit," Coyote replied, as he slowly pulled himself up, "I've got a full pack of guns and ammo stashed near the gate."

Kid stood up and rubbed his arms. "Come on, Tues, leave 'em behind."

"Hey . . . listen to you, the little pacifist."

"Fuck off," Kid challenged. He walked away and put his hands on his hips. He was surprised by his retort.

Coyote moved over to where Kid was standing. "It's a good thing you stayed out of this war, Kid. You would have never made it." He pushed a finger into his chest. "You would have got the first bullet. They like nice guys like you." He laughed, and punched Kid on the arm. "All of the good guys get killed, and the assholes live on to make more wars."

Kid could feel the point in his chest where Coyote had touched. It felt hot. He started to back away, but then stopped himself. He could hear some of the guards running along the paths—their heavy weapons and bandoliers clanking against their bodies—shouts and heavy breathing. "Have you forgotten, Coyote, that you're a Holy Person?"

Coyote scratched his head and bit into his lower lip. "I really can't remember."

Kid stepped back. "Why don't you try?"

"Because war's going on, asshole."

Kid jammed his forehead with the butt of his hand. "Then confiscate a helicopter."

"I would, except they've all been destroyed," Coyote answered harshly. He looked over to where he thought the trailhead might be. "Where you taking Molly?"

"I don't know. Maybe to Paris," he answered facetiously. "Who knows."

Coyote tossed Kid the pack of cigarettes. "Here, you might need these in Paris, Holy Man."

The package landed at his feet. He picked them up and stuffed them in the kimono pocket. "I meant to ask you where you got these smokes."

Coyote laughed. "From the guards, Kid, after you put them to sleep with that little piccolo you made." He waved to his brother. "See you in paradise."

Kid heard him limp up the trail. "S'long Tues." He felt the cellophane package. "Give my best to Ava," he said softly.

Coyote waved. "Sure thing." He stopped and turned around. "You got any drugs?"

"Coyote," Kid replied, "to roughly quote your favorite painter, 'you are drugs.'"

* * * * *

Twice, after packing only the barest of necessities, Molly jerked them out of the bag and put them away. "What right do I have to leave?" she asked herself over and over again. I'm needed at Wandering Foot, and if Kid really loves me he should be able to wait. But, what if he's killed? Or I? Or, if he became fed up with the whole mess and left for home?" Once again, she packed the bag. They would have to leave by canoe which meant going through five sets of rapids. Almost impossible in an open canoe. She sat down on the zabuton and tried to think it through one more time. Immediately she was back up. She was going. "Damn the war and all of those who revolve in that consciousness," she shouted. "There has to be a better way and I'm going to find it."

She turned out the lights, took one last look around her villa and went out the back door. She still had an hour or more to wait. At that moment it seemed like a year.

* * * * *

One mile up the trail to the Aerie Coyote stopped to lean against an unlighted kasuga-dora. He was surprised that Ava had put a lantern there, but then he remembered that she had used them as mile-markers. "Damn," he mumbled to himself, "and this is only the first one." He found a stick to use as a cane, but it didn't seem to help. He was also hungry. "At this rate," he thought, "I'll never be able to make it in time." He closed his eyes and his whole inside world started to spin. Quickly, he grabbed the stone. "Whoa there, Coyote," he mumbled to himself, "there's no one tougher than you, or smarter, right?" He laughed, and started to walk. "Or more fucked up."

* * * * *

Watching her Fifth Mesa monitor, Spider Woman saw the difficulty Coyote was having on the trail. "Oh, that poor thing," she said to herself, as she tried to adjust the picture. "Look at him, Leonardo. I don't think he'll make it." She looked over her shoulder. "Hey da Vinci," she shouted, "can't you tear yourself away from that painting long enough to see what's happening with Tuesday?"

Leonardo put down his brushes, wiped his hands on an oily rag and hobbled over to where Spider Woman was seated. "I can't wait until I have my own studio."

"So what makes you so special?"

"Because I'm da Vinci, that's why."

Spider Woman rocked back and shook both hands like ragdolls. "And we're just a bunch of slobs."

"I didn't mean that." He quickly tried to make amends by looking at the screen. "Oh yeah . . . there he is."

"Listen, mister big shot, if it wasn't for me you'd still be living on the Fourth Mesa with all of those old flared nostril Heavenites. See what matriarchy can do for you." She tapped the monitor. "Now take a good look at what Tuesday Coyote is doing.

Leonardo, feeling somewhat defeated, peered into the screen. "My oh my, Spider Woman, he appears half dead, and the other half looks drastically hung over." He lovingly touched her arm. "What's the score?"

"You ain't watching no ballgame, Leonardo, you're seeing a young Holy Person about to croak." She stood up and put her arms around his waist. "I thought you might be able to help him."

"How?"

Spider Woman shook her head. "You invented the helicopter . . . right?"

"It's in the shop."

"Well, hot shot, get it out . . ."

"But I'm almost finished with my new Mona Lisa." He walked back to his easel. "The light's so poor in here."

"Do this for me and I'll see what I can do about getting you a new studio," Spider Woman said.

Leonardo picked up a brush and dipped it into the burnt umber.

"Leonardo," Spider Woman said, quietly, "famous painter and inventor that you are, how would you like to shack up for the rest of your life with Ms Nuclear Spud? Just try and get some sweet loving from her." She stepped over to his easel. "Or, maybe Porch Swing and be mesmerized back into the corn belt." She slowly started putting his brushes into a canvas bag. "Or," she continued,

"Beethoven's Fourth. All day and night you get to listen to that almost as famous as you concerto. No rock an' roll, no jazz, no Baroque, or Post Classical, or Nat King Cole."

"All right, all right," Leonardo yelled, as he grabbed his flight jacket and put on an old leather football helmet. "I keep hearing how badly I'm pussywhipped." He found his flight boots and jerked them on.

"Well, you could also live in the bachelor quarters and listen to Swiss Army Knife go through his studly twelve blades routine." She pulled out a large trunk from under the bed. "Here, take these to Coyote." She started pulling out some neatly ironed clothes. "He really looks ridiculous in that silly looking bathrobe. She put them in a wicker basket. "Oh yes, here are his boots, hat and concho belt. These clothes will make him feel much better." She kissed Leonardo on the cheek. "Please be careful, and you'd better keep this little operation under your oversized hat. I'm sure The Great Mother wouldn't approve."

"Well poop on Mona," Leonardo replied, as he removed the clothes from the basket and stuffed them into his flight bag. He stuck the large brimmed hat over his helmet. "Well, here I go again, off to save your world."

"Just for that, ace, you just won Nuclear Spud as your bed partner."

"I'm going mama," Leonardo said, as he ducked through the door, "the whiz kid's on his way."

*　　*　　*　　*　　*

Kid didn't have any trouble finding the trail, but one hundred yards past Molly's villa it was so overgrown that he kept turning the wrong way. He slowed down, and then realized that he could guide himself by using the stone path. After that, it became easier as he pushed his way through the vegetation. As long as the stones continued he would be all right. After what seemed to be an extremely long time, he stumbled onto a boat dock. He carefully stepped up and immediately tripped on an overturned canoe. "Damn," he cursed, as he grabbed his shin and looked for the Shoin. He noticed a light shining through the trees. "Molly," he shouted. The river noise was too loud. He tried again. "Hey . . . Molly!" He could hardly hear his own voice. Still, there was no response. Slowly, he worked his way through the ferns until he found the stairs. Cautiously, he tried the first step. It groaned as if it were alive. He quickly moved to the next one. "Molly," he yelled. "It's me . . . Kid."

Slowly, he ascended the stairs until he came to the first landing. "Molly . . ."

Suddenly a light appeared. "Kid?"

"Yeah . . . it's me."

She stepped down to the landing. "Kid, I'm so glad you made it."

He touched her face. "I was worried that you wouldn't be here." He gently kissed her lips. "I missed you."

Surprised, she looked into his face, and then leaned against him. Kid kissed the top of her head. She looked up and smiled. "Kid, I'm so excited." She kissed his cheek. "And frightened."

He wrapped his arms around her. "Coyote's on his way to the Aerie."

"Is he okay?"

"I'm not sure." He lifted up her chin and kissed her mouth.

"Kid," Molly whispered, as she continued to squeeze him as tightly as she could. "May told me that she was going to send the three of you to the front."

"We'll be long gone . . ." He kissed her again. "Hopefully." He took her hands and looked around the corner. "Can we stay here until first light?"

Molly led him up the stairs and onto a narrow deck. "I think we'll be safe."

Kid jumped up and down on the deck. "It feels solid enough."

"Oh, it's still in wonderful condition, Kid. I've been using the Shoin for a long time." She grabbed his hand and pulled him through the door. "I want you to see this sandpainting I've been working on." Kid followed her into the one room cabin. Molly closed the shutters as Kid stepped into the center of the room.

"Whoa . . . what's this?"

Molly put the lamps down on the floor. "It's my contribution to peace." She laughed, and shook her head as she glanced at Kid. "I feel embarrassed. It sounds so funny to say it." She swept her arm over a circular sandpainting. "This is it . . . my peace."

Kid slowly walked around the large sandpainting. It's brilliant colors sparkled in the soft light. Molly kept ahead of Kid—looking as if she were seeing it for the first time. She stopped, and pointed to the center figure which she called Buddha Shooting Way. He sat protected inside a white circle. She walked him through the rest of the sandpainting. There was Pollen Boy in one corner, Jesus in another, and opposite were Holy Man and Holy Woman. She had the Four Winds in black, yellow, blue, and red stripes, and Confucius and Lao-tsu were dancing inside the feathers that surrounded the central figure. Around the border Martin Luther's Dream speech was written in copper and turquoise sand. Molly knelt down and picked up a handful of red sandstone powder. "I've been secretly working on this for a long time."

Kid continued to walk around the piece until he finally settled down on a tatami mat opposite Molly. Off to one side were jars filled with the materials she had used: ground cinnabar, turquoise, azurite, lapis, malachite, sandstone, granite, charcoal, silver, gold, copper, powdered sea shells and some ground colored glass. He touched each of the different materials. "It's absolutely amazing." He looked up and grinned. "You've got most of the heavyweights from the Seventh Mesa."

Molly felt embarrassed. "Well . . . I . . . ah . . ." She lowered her eyes and smiled. "Someday, perhaps this will really work." She laughed, and brushed Pollen Boy's blond hair. "This is my own Hall of Fame."

Kid laughed. "What do you call it?"

"What would you call it?" she asked.

He looked at Molly's creation for a long time. Finally, he broke out in a spontaneous smile. "How about Zenout at the Third Hogan Shalom."

"That's wonderful," she exclaimed. "These Tibetan and Navajo writings are a prophecy about world peace." She tapped her fingers together. "So, I have chosen Buddha Shooting Way to bring them to the Third Mesa." She pointed to the central character. "A male and female being who possesses the female powers of sensibility and sensitivity, and the male strengths and stamina. She or he, depending upon the circumstances, is the final balacing act. The creative and the receptive all charged together in a kinetic field of vision." She looked up at Kid. "I call it . . . Gandhi Dancer." She laughed and shrugged. "Gandhi's all this negative space . . . like the soft brown earth."

Kid smiled. Nodding his head as he slowly stood up and stepped back. "Gandhi Dancer," he said quietly to himself.

Molly's eyes looked as if the sandpainting was reflected in each one. "And now these High Holy People live here with us." She took a deep breath. "I think of God only as peace. Nothing else. I can't go beyond that." She picked up one of the lamps. "Let's go out on the deck. It is so quiet, and the guns have stopped. See, I've made a place for us." She took his hand and presented him the bed.

He looked almost embarrassed. "Whoa . . . ," he said, as he looked into her eyes. "Now, if we only had the moon as our witness." He sighed. "It must be wonderful here in the daytime."

Molly put Kid's hand around her waist. "When I'm here I feel as though I've been painted into a Japanese landscape. Of all the magical places at Wandering Foot this is my favorite. Because it can take me to so many other wonderful places in my mind. She leaned against him. "Someday Kid, perhaps years and years from now, tourists will come to Wandering Foot and they'll be shown this Shoin where Third Mesa peace was first created." She laughed and put her head on his shoulder. "Gandhi Dancer will be here of course, and the guides will tell stories about you and me and how we had to escape in this little boat through five monsterous sets of rapids, over Double Lightning Falls, past the Fourth Mesa until we found our own little home where we had lots of babies, and many years later, after Wandering Foot was healed, we came back and started all over again." She threw her hands into the air. "Ta dum . . . !"

Kid turned around and took a deep breath. "How many kids?" He knelt down on the futon.

Molly stepped over the bed and sat down. "About five thousand . . . at least." She fluffed up two pillows. "If, m'lord, we intend to create a whole new Third Mesa mojo."

Kid scooted next to her. "I think you've been talking with my mother."

"Mona . . ."

Kid laughed, and slipped his arm around her.

Molly lowered the wick. "I've never spent a night with a man before. At least, not this way." She pinched Kid's cheek. "And here I am with a man who has probably made love with every Holy Person on the Fifth Mesa."

Kid laughed,and snuggled his head into her hair. "That doesn't count."

"What!" Molly yelled, as she sat up. "What's this I'm hearing from you. Male crappola!"

Kid slid down and grabbed a pillow for protection. "Now hold your fire, Molly Rose, and listen to me." He sat up just in case he had to dodge her punches. "Tues hasn't made love with a woman in eight years, but he's probably killed at least . . . I don't know . . . a lot." He moved closer. "Which would you prefer?"

"I would prefer, Mister Monday, that you put away that pillow." Molly moved over and slapped the futon. "Just about right here is good enough." Kid came closer. "Don't be afraid, Kid."

He reached over and touched her lips with his fingertip. "I had a dream about you last night." He sat up and shook his head. "Have I only been here one night?"

"I've heard that you Holy People have no sense of time."

He looked at Molly, smiled, and then kissed her. "But I've been in love with you for a long time."

Molly put her arms around him. "I hope you're right, Kid." She kissed him back. "I had the feeling that you thought of me as a little kid." She kissed him again. "Do you remember that model airplane you made for me?"

"Sure," he answered, "it was a Sopwith Camel."

"I've always wanted to learn how to fly one of those biplanes." She scooted onto the pillow. "How would that look on my resumé?" She sat up and crossed her legs. "Listen to this." She started waving her arms as if she were conducting an orchestra. "The young woman, Molly Rose, wife of Kid Monday and mother of thousands, who all by herself created world peace with her amazing, all-purpose, stay-pressed five-d sandpainting, flies to all of the international peace festivals in her vintage Sopwith Camel. And now, because she has finally been ordained a true-blue left-handed cosmic Holy Person, she intends to live on the Fifth Mesa, and maybe . . . if she can pull it off, the Seventh Mesa to get away from her mother-in-law, with her husband, Kid Happy-Go-Lucky Monday and all of their snotnosed brats." She punched Kid on the arm. "How does that sound?"

"I think you're lacking in self confidence."

"What do you expect for the daughter of an Apache freedom fighter and a Tibetan shaman? She pinned his arms. "I bet you can't throw me off."

Kid pulled her down on top of him. "You just might be the choreographer of world peace, baby, but you sure don't know much about making love."

She lifted up her head. "These things take time, Kid, give me a break. I'm just an innocent virgin who's only made it in her dreams."

"And by the way it's going, you'll probably be a virgin for a long time."

Molly hooted, and licked his face. "How's this?"

"Wonderful."

"I thought it just might turn you on." She kissed his nose.

A lone coyote started howling up on the rim. Molly sat up and listened. "Is that your brother?" she asked, as she folded her body around him.

"Yes, and he's cheering for us."

"I hope so, Kid, because I need all the help I can get." She kissed his neck.

"I think you already have it, Molly."

"Really?"

"You're already flying with the Gandhi Dancer, baby . . ."

After Mona had spent the morning working on her biography with The Cowboy Buddha, she joined some of the Third Mesa children on the com- **11** puter center's deck. Overnight, the cherry trees had bloomed, and there were also large tubs of tulips, daffodils, crocuses and hyacinths surrounding each table. Fruit smoothies had been served for a midmorning treat. Mona sat down with Rosie. "Hiya," she said, as she put her arm around the girl. The Great Mother was dressed in white silk shorts, baby blue leotard, a light cashmere pink sweater and a new pair of white aerobic shoes she was testing for the manufacturer.

Rosie acted surprised. "Well, okay I guess."

"That's good," Mona answered.

Jamal came running over from the main computer room. "Hey Mona," he shouted excitedly, as he skidded to a stop, "The Whoa Man said that some of the Holy Highs from the Seventh Mesa are missing."

Mona leaned back and peered into the room. "For how long?"

Jamal shrugged. "He didn't say."

"Which ones?" Rosie asked.

Jamal sat down, rolled his eyes, took a quick breath and then began to count off their names. "There's Buddha Shooting Way, Gandhi, Pollen Boy, Lao-tsu . . ."

"Which one's Loud Sue?" the youngest girl, Lisa, asked as she sipped her drink."

Mona laughed and wrapped her arms around her. "His name is Lao-tsu. Lao as in Tao."

Rosie, who had gone to the main room, came hurriedly back. "The Whoa Man says we can't find them anywhere."

"Why not?" She stood up.

Rosie shrugged. "I don't know." She backed away.

Mona saw how intimidated she was. She put her arm on her shoulder. "I'm sorry, Rosie . . ."

LaMar joined Rosie and Jamal. "They've jammed our computers," he said. He elbowed Jamal. "That's what The Whoa Man thinks." He stepped closer. "With their psychic powers."

Mona closed her eyes and tried to think. "Why?" she asked herself.

LaMar leaned against the table. He seemed to be all arms and legs. "He also said that Leonardo's on his way to the Third Mesa in your new helicopter."

"All right," Jamal shouted, as he snapped his fingers. "He's going to help Coyote, right?" He flipped out both thumbs. "That's hot."

Mona grabbed Jamal's neck and pulled him against her muscular body. "I'll hot you, kiddo," she said, as she knuckled his hair, "that's my helicopter."

"Hey," he shouted, as he tried to squirm away, "he's helping your son get back with his wife."

"Leonardo flies like an old lady," Mona answered, as she started to tickle him.

Sensing the dramatic change in Mona's personality, Jamal tried to tickle her back. "You mean like you . . ."

Mona grabbed his wrist, quickly flipped his arm behind his back and pushed him into the computer room. "We've got a bunch of big mouths around here," she said, as she stopped in front of the computer. "I suggest that you have some respect for us old farts." Without thinking, she kissed him on the cheek and let him go. He ran off shaking his arm.

The Whoa Man, who was standing next to the computer, dropped his clipboard. "Whoa . . . what's this?"

"How come The Great Mother's being so friendly?" LaMar asked Spider Woman and April Fools who had just arrived from the Seventh Mesa.

April Fools shrugged. "What's going on?"

Heidi pointed toward Mona. "I don't know, but suddenly she's talking and playing around with us."

April Fools looked over at Spider Woman. "Dat Whoaman's no longer got dee blues."

Heidi, having overheard his comment, stepped between him and Spider Woman. "I think she's finally worked off every ounce of body fat and now she doesn't know what to do."

"If she gets any younger looking," Spider Woman added, "she'll go through puberty again."

The Great Mother put her arms around LaMar and Rosie and spoke to the computer. "We want every Third Mesa monitor turned on." The screens came on and Mona quickly examined all twenty-four of them. "Okay . . . take ten, thirteen, twenty-five and that's . . . okay . . . let's also have seventeen." Carefully, she examined her choices. "Yes . . . that's enough." Twenty screens went dark. Mona looked over at The Whoa Man. "When did this happen?"

"Well, just a short time ago," he answered.

"Why didn't he ask me?" she questioned.

The Whoa Man fiddled with his clipboard. "Well . . . ah . . . I guess . . ."

"Because," April Fools said, as he moved closer to Mona, "he's afraid of you."

"What?" Mona asked Spider Woman. "Is this true?"

Spider Woman nodded, "Yes . . ." She moved closer to Mona. "He didn't think you would understand."

"About going to help my own son?" Mona questioned.

Spider Woman nodded.

Mona turned back to the screens. "It's still dark on the Third Mesa . . . right?" She checked her computer. "Leonardo will be flying the canyon at night." She studied the four screens. "Put them onto one screen," she ordered the computer.

The four separate images were transformed onto a larger screen. There were two shots of Coyote and Leonardo inside the helicopter, one outside the helicopter and the fourth one was of the Aerie.

"Tuesday looks horrible," Mona said quietly. She shook her head. It was the first time in years that she had seen her son. "I can't believe how much older he looks than Kid." She turned to Spider Woman. "I can't watch."

Spider Woman felt a warmth permeate her body. "I know . . ."

"Look at Leonardo fly through the canyon," Jamal said. "That's bitchin'."

"What did you expect, dummy," Rosie challenged, "he invented the helicopter."

"Yeah," April Fools interjected, "but his design looked like a buffalo scrotum with hyperactive dragonfly wings."

"Hey, how about some sound?" Heidi asked.

The Whoa Man flipped a switch and immediately picked up Coyote's and Leonardo's conversation through the sound of the chopper blades.

Mona stepped back. "I can't watch this," she said to Spider Woman, "Tues looks so hurt." She closed her eyes. "It's too painful." She touched Spider Woman's arm. "I'll be in my chalet. Please tell me what happens to them." She turned and left the room. "See you . . . kids." She looked back and waved.

"Why is she leaving?" LaMar asked.

"Shhhhhh . . . ," Spider Woman said.

The Whoa Man adjusted the sound. Leonardo's voice came over the speakers. He had just picked up Coyote and they were hovering over the trail.

"Where are we going?" Leonardo asked. Coyote was rubbing his bad leg.

Coyote pointed up. "To the Aerie," he answered. He looked over at his godfather. "It's about five thousand feet."

Leonardo nodded, as he spun the chopper's nose around and started to climb. "Getting back with Ava?"

A smile broke through his pain. "I'm not sure what I'm doing, Leonardo. Trying to find a warm bed, save my tired ass, or what?"

"I know the feeling, Tues." The chopper sliced across the canyon as Leonardo kept one eye on the instruments and the other checking the canyon wall.

Coyote tried to see the Aerie. "Do you have one of those silencers for this bird?"

Leonardo studied the instruments. His long gray beard was tucked inside his jacket. Coyote's hat was still over the helmet.

"Ahhh . . . here we go," he said as he flipped the switch. "In my day we called this mode, pianissimo." He laughed and glanced over at Coyote. "It has a classic sound to it, don't you think?"

The helicopter noise was completely eliminated. "That's much better," Coyote said as he closed his eyes.

"Did I ever tell you that I met Ava's father one time?" Leonardo said. "What an artist."

Coyote laughed. "Yeah . . . you mentioned that."

"The man's a pure genius and I can't imagine why he isn't up there on the Seventh Mesa."

Coyote slid down in his seat as far as he could go. The last thing he wanted to discuss was Mesa politics. "How's Spider Woman?" he asked.

Leonardo smiled. "Good," he answered. "She sends her love."

"And Mom?" Coyote's eyes closed.

"Ahhh . . . our Mona." Leonardo slapped Coyote's knee. "She's been having a difficult time since the moon incident."

"Yeah, Kid told me," Coyote answered, as he quickly sat up and shook away a yawn. "We should be getting close. He looked out the window. "Yes, there's a light."

Leonardo could hardly make out the Aerie's shape. "Where do you want to be deposited?"

"If you could just take it up a little more then I could drop out above the hut." He reached back for the rope ladder. "I'd like to surprise Ava."

"You sound just like a man sneaking back home." Leonardo turned the chopper one hundred and eighty degrees.

"You're right on target, Leonardo," Coyote said. He opened the door. "Thanks for the help, and please give my love to Spider Woman." He reached over and shook his godfather's hand.

"Hey!" Leonardo shouted, "I almost forgot." He handed Coyote the bag of clothes and took off the black Navajo hat. "Spider Woman sent these for you."

"I thought that chapeau looked familiar." Coyote tucked the bag under his arm and jammed the hat onto his head. "You're not goin' to get into trouble for this, are you?"

Leonardo flicked the front of his helmet. "Well Tues, I'll have to face up to your mom, but that's a heck of a lot better than dealing with Spider Woman." He laughed and slapped Coyote's shoulder. "She almost had me living with Nuclear Spud."

Coyote dropped the bag and started to climb down the ladder. "It's tough being a true Renaissance Man . . . ain't it?"

Leonardo burst into laughter. "You've got that right." He waved, and hauled in the ladder after Coyote had reached the ground. "See ya, Tues . . ."

Spider Woman turned off the moniters.

"Hey," April Fools shouted. "Why'd you do that?"

"I'm keeping you from becoming a voyeur," Spider Woman replied. "Can't you find anything else to occupy your warped mind?"

"All right, my dearest Victorian double-chocolate pound cake, how about this?" He went over to the computer and read a printout about what was happening on the Third Mesa. "Hey you guys, Kid is spending the night with Molly."

"That's it," Spider Woman shouted, as she grabbed a broom and started pushing him out the door. "Get out of here." She ran out everyone except The Whoa Man who was working on an experiment to clone the Seventh Mesa's consciousness and then have it reincarnated back to the Third Mesa. Spider Woman looked at his calculations. "Did you steal the Holy Highs from the Seventh Mesa?"

The Whoa Man didn't answer as he was clearing his mind to process her question. Eventually he looked up. "Hmmmmm . . . I guess I can 't clone them if they're not where I need them to be, can I?" He adjusted his glasses and scratched his head. "Right?"

Spider Woman laughed. She was feeling much better since The Great Mother seemed to be coming out of her depression. She touched The Whoa Man's soft hands. "Yo . . . !"

$$* \quad * \quad * \quad * \quad *$$

Coyote opened one eye and cautiously scanned the open room. Books, paintings, a large work table, handwoven rugs over a waxed floor. He sat up and shook his head as if he could not remember where he was, or how he had arrived. It was all so fuzzy. He looked out the window at the opposite rim. A streak of light had cut across the horizon like a pale blue sword. He checked his computer and he was surprised that it had only been a few hours since Leonardo had dropped him above the Aerie. He listened for noises, but all he heard was a strange ringing in his ears which he interpreted as one of his many war injuries. He stood up and immediately sat back down. His right leg felt like it had become a rusty steel rod. "Whoa there," he moaned. "Hang tough, ol' boy." Suddenly, he smelled coffee. He sniffed, and the aroma forced him to close his eyes. "Ava," a voice said somewhere inside.

Coyote stood up again and started toward the kitchen. "Ava," he said out loud.

A tall, suntanned woman stepped into the room. There was a wide knowing smile that told him she knew all along they would eventually be together. Her features were mixed in such a way that it was almost impossible to imagine her ethnic background: possibly black, or perhaps East Indian. Or . . . maybe Middle Eastern. Her hair was kinky blond and her eyes were Titanic green. High cheekbones, large eyes, her lips looked as if they had been brushed with Himalyan gold. A perfect Matisse-Post Impression. She was dressed in a well worn, neatly pressed jumpsuit. The uniform of a prisoner.

She moved.

He moved.

They stopped.

"I thought . . ."

"You . . ."

Ava took Coyote's hands and gently pulled him into her arms. "I was told that you had been killed."

"You should know better . . ."

She turned him around. His right foot caught the edge of a wool rag rug and he stumbled. "Oh, I'm sorry," she said.

He sat down on a chair. "That's okay." He looked up. "Old war wound."

"That's what they all say . . ." She knelt down and rubbed his knee. "I was searching for you when I was captured." She studied his face—looking for something that she had known before. A lot of it was gone. That young trickster gleam cushioned by pastels of youth. He was hard and lined and it seemed that all of his pain was released in his face. She kissed his cheek. "Eight year . . . ?"

Coyote leaned back in the chair. "You look exactly the same."

"Come on, Coyote, are you trying to promote me into the sack?" She touched her breasts. "My tits sag . . ."

Coyote grabbed his crotch. "My balls droop . . ."

Looks like we're about even." She walked into the small kitchen. "I was making coffee."

"Coffee," he answered, in a low coarse voice. "You mean the real honest-to-god, low down, fat bottomed kickass coffee that . . ."

"The very same." She laughed, and stepped sideways over to

93

the small propane stove. "The beans have been here all this time. I had them in my secret hideout. No one found them."

"You could stop the war with a handful of those little snot-nosed buggers," he said, as he stood up.

"Or start another." She filled two cups. "There's no cream, but I do have a few cubes of sugar."

Immediately, Coyote put up one hand. "Don't mess with it, Ava . . . I just want to keep it dirty." He took a deep breath. "Wow," he remarked, "it's like a body-blow . . . whooompffff."

Ava leaned against the sink. He looked like a stranger to her but felt like an old friend. She was confused. She dropped a lump of sugar into a large cup and slowly stirred as she watched Coyote take his first sip. He made her feel happy that she could give him such a simple gift. He looked up from having his nose down in the cup. "Kid's down there," he said, almost inaudibly. "He's trying to get Molly out." He took a second sip. Already, he could feel the caffeine begin its velvet seduction. "I bummed a ride up here with Leonardo." He carefully put down the cup. "Y'know, Spider Woman's old man."

"Ahhhh . . . in his old helicopter."

"No, he ripped off Mom's."

"How is your mother?"

"She's changed her name to Mona." He slowly shook his head. "She no longer wants to be the Great Mom." He looked up and caught an iridescence in the way she watched him. "I . . . ah . . . heard that you were taken to Wandering Foot." He glanced down at the boots that Spider Woman had sent with Leonardo. "I had to see you."

"I'm sorry," she replied, as she noticed Coyote's old boots. For a few seconds she was silent and then she looked up. "I'm sorry that I took sides."

The sound of her voice told him that everything had been forgiven. The years of war had caused an erosion of simple, clear thinking which left an equation that was fortified with weapons and hatred. Ava had been swept up into a woman's defense, and by trying to change the male consciousness she became just that. They were slowly moving closer. "I hated you back then," he said softly.

"I wished for your balls on a rustly skewer."

Coyote laughed. "I think you managed . . ."

Ava looked into Coyote's eyes. "No . . ."

"Close enough . . . baby."

"I saw you limping."

"I took some shrapnel." He patted his right leg.

"Anything more?"

Coyote thought about the eight years of celibacy, but decided not to say anything. "Once, I was strung out on opium but now booze is my only real fun."

"I have a little brandy," Ava said, as she opened one of the cabinets.

"Are you kidding?" he asked. "My wounds would sell my soul for just a little sip."

Ava reached into a cupboard and took out a pint of brandy. "Here . . ." She took off the cap. "Say when." Coyote held up his hand after she had brought it to the top.

"I'm starting to drool," he said.

Ava set the bottle down and put her hands on Coyote's shoulders. "You dear, crazy roadrunner." She kissed his cheek. "Ahhh . . ." she murmured, "you still smell like sweet sage and rainy days."

"I only smell the war."

"I know those smells, Tues, and you ain't got them." She rubbed her fingers over his cheek. "I'm slowly beginning to find my memory of you." She kissed him once more." She took his hand. "Let's sit down." She picked up the porcelain pot, and motioned for Coyote to bring in the tray with some cheese and crackers.

Coyote set the tray on a low table and looked out the front window. Seven miles down, Wandering Foot was like an island floating in his mind. Suddenly, the southern breezes came up and the Aerie swayed and groaned as it seemed to translate the wind blowing from the other mesas. "Ahhh . . . those mortals down there," he said jokingly, "how they can mess things up."

"And we used to think how enlightened we were," Ava replied. "Remember?"

Coyote ducked his head and winced. "We danced all night with that illusion." He sat on a wooden frame that held a futon. Ava was seated on the floor. "But you . . . are not an illusion." He wanted to join her but he couldn't. She leaned against the wall and picked up a cracker. "I can remember how we believed that the only fences we'd ever need were miles of azalea hedgerows."

"And we ended up with barbed-wire." She snapped her fingers. "Just like that." She glanced out the window. "And now, for some strange reason, my being requires two guards day and night."

"I can tell that you are a dangerous woman."

"I must be to May." She looked back at Coyote. "A few years ago I challenged her leadership. I was fed up with the war, and I believed it could be stopped. I was hearing all kinds of rebellious chatter and complaints about May and her staff, but when it came right down to the showdown, I lost."

"Is that when you took off for the desert?"

"I was forced into the desert." She emptied the last of the coffee into Coyote's cup. "No one thought I would survive."

"You were lucky . . ."

"No, I was good." She laughed. "Damn good. It was only when I got into the mountains that I got picked up by . . . ," she looked at Coyote, "your men. I asked for you, but I was told that you were on some secret mission." She pushed the plate closer to her husband. "They kept telling me that you were, hands down, the finest soldier they'd ever seen." She closed her eyes and took a long, deep breath. "That scared me more than anything I had heard before."

Coyote shook his head. "I lost my soul out there, Ava." He motioned toward the window. "My heart, my mind and any love that I once had for myself." He clenched his hands and quickly opened them. "Everything went dead."

"The male psyche gone beserk," Ava said, almost inaudibly. She touched Coyote's rough hands. "I'm so glad you escaped."

Coyote searched her face for what it was he had come for: hope, peace and a sanctuary within her heart. It was all there. He could see it and it made him feel much better. "Me too," he remarked. He rubbed her hands as if he were trying to absorb their warmth. He looked up. "When I was out there . . ." He jerked his head toward the south rim, "what made me feel happy, what made me laugh a little was our old skydiving adventures." He laughed. "Now that was something else."

Ava stood up and walked to the window. "We were hot . . . right?" She leaned against the bookcase. "Total abandonment. It was like we were two different people." She touched his shoulder. "When we were barn storming around the Third Mesa—county fairs, half-times at halfwit sports events, bullshit political rallies, weddings, circumcisions, hooplas and fandangos." She reached under the couch and pulled out a large scrapbook. "We were, Tuesday Coyote, a couple of skydiving fools."

96

Coyote seemed amazed that she was so animated about their old adventures. "I'm surprised that . . . ."

"Me too." She opened the book. "I felt so spiritual in such a non-spiritual way." She shrugged. "Hey, look at this, Tues." She ran a finger over a newspaper photograph. "A Double Helix G-Force-5 Sixty-nine with a Parabolic Glide for a landing. No one, and I mean no one . . . baby . . . has even been able to duplicate that move."

"Hey, we won the entire purse . . . right?" He stared at the clipping. "I do remember."

Ava flipped the page. "Sure we did. Listen to this, Tues, 'Ava Matisse and Tuesday Coyote have revolutionized championship skydiving.'" Ava looked at Coyote. "That reviewer got it right."

"We sure had sting back then, didn't we?" He looked into her dark green eyes.

"Sting . . . ?" Ava questioned. "You call that sting?" She put down the book and stood up. "Baby, we were floating in the pocket of God. We could do no wrong. We were shooting the heavenly rapids, baby, and we had full-blown, turbo charged love riding with us." She moved a small coffee table over to the wall. "And you know what? Of all the moves we had, not once did we ever try to make love in flight." She laughed, and grabbed his hands. "Can you imagine that? Not once." She leaned back and started to spin with Coyote. "We would make love all night, but then, when we got up there . . . it was all business." She saw that Coyote was having a hard time keeping up. "Oh, I'm sorry Tues."

He skipped around as he tried to work the pain out of his leg. "You're absolutely right," he answered. He looked around and found a long mauve silk scarf that Spider Woman had woven for Ava. He threw it around his neck. "I can feel it, Ava . . . just like it was before. Only this time we're doing it in the privacy of our own hemisphere." He backed up and placed his hands against the wall. "Okay . . . we're twenty thousand feet . . . no . . . make it thirty so we'll have more time for a little foreplay, and we jump out of this beautiful thirsty orange Apache skyhawk, and we have a free fall of twenty-nine thousand feet before we have to pull our anti-celibacy chutes. We slide out of our down-filled cabooses, and swing over to each other for a little romp in the tropospheric hay. We make love once, twice, maybe even three times, and Ba-Ba-Bawhooooom, our chutes open with fireworks shooting out from all of our Post Modern orifices and we land right in the center of everyone's buttermilk pancakes. Now, the judges get so turned on that they're hugging and kissing each other, everyone in the stands has climbed into each other's mouths, and there is so much universal zippity-do-dah that the entire Third Mesa is swamped in the giant breath of One Come Humping, or . . . maybe it was One Hump Coming."

"Oh Tues, except for the fact that you look as if you've eaten the last ten years all by yourself, you haven't changed a bit." She kissed his cheek. "Was that demonstration what you might call a proposition?"

"It's a Flying Holy Hail Chant as we kick in our mescalito afterburners, and we're joined by Buddha Two Shoes and East Jesus Ray Ban for the grand finale in our East Meets West competition to determine how many Hail Marys are required to pass a Hopi through the Vatican's uprights."

Ava was smiling. She could not believe that they were acting as though they had never separated. She watched Coyote wipe his brow, and then hobble into the kitchen for the bottle. "I had this dream a few nights ago, Coyote, and in it we had jumped out of an old biplane. It was something like we were supposed to be making love although the flight lasted all night long. Over and over again as we slowly began to change into this incredible white flower like a lotus. We grew larger and larger and more beautiful as it slowly consumed our bodies until there was nothing left but this pure opalescence that gradually turned into the moon."

Coyote had stopped pouring as he watched Ava. He too was amazed that they fit so easily. It almost made him nervous, and he questioned why it had taken so long. Why they had allowed for their lives to be captured by the war. It would have been so easy to leave it alone. Walk away. It was probably the true coyote in him, he thought. His fascination to juggle the mystical alligators fed on high octane fuel at the piranha school of sunday brunch.

"Coyote," Ava said, as she touched the bottle. "Where did you go?"

Coyote came to, finished off the drink, and took Ava's hand. "Looks like we're in the same hoosegow . . ."

Ava jammed her hands into her pockets. "I was told to be ready at six."

Coyote looked at his computer. "We've got exactly fifteen minutes." He took a long swallow from the bottle. "Let's give them a good run for their money." He motioned toward the back of the

Aerie. "Didn't you put in an escape clause somewhere," he said, just in case I came looking for you way back when?"

"There's a secret trail that leads to the Fifth Mesa."

Coyote smiled. "That's what I thought."

"If we're caught we'll be shot."

"If we go down we'll be shot."

"Perhaps we can hook up with Molly and Kid. At least there will be four of us." She touched Coyote's leg. "Can you make it?"

"We have no choice." He carefully put on his black hat with the beaded headband. "We just might be able to sneak along the Fifth Mesa and come out where I think we'll find Kid and Molly. At Double Lightning Falls."

Ava hurried into the kitchen and proceeded to fill a rucksack with as much food as she could find: cheese, crackers, canned meat. "This will last us a few days." She looked over at Coyote. "I've got some medical supplies."

"Pain killers . . . ?"

"Only a small tin of aspirin."

"Forget it." He put the photo album into the pack. "Someday, we just might need a few reminders as to how great we were back then."

Ava pulled out the entire casing of a recessed shelving. On the other side steps had been cut into a sandstone wall. "I thought I was being paranoid when I made this passageway."

"Always have an escape route, Ava. Animals know that best. Especially, Doctor Coyote." A thin shaft of light came down through the narrow passage.

"Ah . . . smell the fresh air."

"Right from the Fifth Mesa, my dear." Coyote shouldered the pack. "Careful, after what we've been through, it could make us instantly holy."

"Yo!" Ava exclaimed, "Now that would be a shame, wouldn't it?" She took Coyote's hand and kissed it. "I had it all planned out that we'd make love the very first thing. Y'know, just to . . ." She kissed him on the lips. "I don't know what." She laughed and put her head against his chest. "Just to make love."

Coyote put his arm around her. "I haven't made love in eight years." His statement, spoken so casually, rocked her back against the door. Instantly, her own sexuality was threatened and the playfulness was gone. He could see that she was stunned as she searched for the right comment. "I don't have a war wound, Ava, nor have I turned gay." He held onto the ladder to take the weight off his leg. "After you split, Ava, I was so blown away that being with another woman was the last thing I wanted. Then, one year of war slid into two, and then it was five, and by that time I had been through so many battles and seen so much killing that the thought of having an intimate relationship with a woman without love seemed obscene. I knew that if I could love someone, if she could love me, then something might happen. But, it didn't, or I avoided it when there was a possibility." He turned to lean the pack against the rungs. "All I wanted was to be with you, make love and have some kids. But, in the absolute horror of it all, you were always the enemy." He closed his eyes and stared into the darkness. "It was a turn-on for most of the men." He shrugged, and thoughtfully opened his eyes. "But," he shook his head, "it never worked for me."

"I'm sorry, Coyote."

"You don't have to be."

"She carefully reached out with her hand and touched his fingers. "We'll take it slow . . ."

"I'm not even sure if that's right. To go slow so that I'll someday come out of this vast nothingness that I'm feeling, or . . . jump right in." He tried to smile but the weariness within him overrode his attempt.

It's all right, Tues. It's okay. Besides, we've got our hands full just trying to keep our top knots." There was a muffled explosion, and then five more were layered on top of each other. "Listen," she said, as she grabbed Coyote's arm, "they're starting again."

"They're shelling Wandering Foot."

Ava kissed Coyote on the lips. "I love you, Tues."

Coyote touched her face and kissed her cheek. "I love you . . . Ava." He adjusted his pack and started up the ladder. "And that's the best sound I've heard in eight years." With each step he was forced to pull his bad leg. "Just keep reminding me, Ava, just keep it up."

"I've got it, I've got it," Kid yelled, as he sat up in bed. First light had just blushed the horizon. Kid was trying to figure out where he was. **12** He felt Molly's body and then leaned over her sleeping face. Her breath smelled of honey and pomegranates. Molly slowly opened her eyes.

"Kid, what's wrong?"

Kid kissed her ear and snuggled his head into her neck. "I'm sorry," he apologized.

"Tell me." Her eyes closed and she grabbed his fingers.

"Well," he said, as he ran his hands down her back, "I had this dream about what we could do until the war ends and Wandering Foot heals itself. It's so simple that I can't believe we didn't think of it sooner." Kid raised his head and looked at her face. She had gone back to sleep. "But," he said, mostly to himself, "I need my trombone."

Molly was determined not to give in to this morning chatter. Her dream was just too good, and she felt so safe. Then she realized that he was leaving and it felt as if he had suddenly been ripped out of her body. She sat up, looked around the

engawa and rubbed her eyes. Kid was leaning against the railing.
"You're stark naked . . ."

Unconcerned, Kid looked at his body. "No, this is one of those
old male God costumes." He pretended to run a zipper up his chest.
"We Mesa-Fivers don't look like you guys at all." He pointed at
Molly's breasts. "See, you've got those bumps . . ."

Molly threw a pillow at him. "I had this dream . . ."

Kid started putting on his clothes. "We really need my trombone . . ."

". . . that we were flying in that little bi-plane you made for me.
I was the pilot and we were zooming over delicious green hills, zipping through apricot clouds . . ."

". . . we're going to Paris . . ."

". . . and we had enough fuel to last forever . . ."

". . . and I overheard one of the guards say that you had Cheyenne . . ."

". . . and we found this valley and all of the Wandering Foot kids
were there . . ."

". . . to hell with it all, we'll just go live in Paris when there was
one . . . say about 1920."

". . . we must get out of here right now, Kid." Molly jumped up.
"What time is it?"

Kid looked at his Fifth Mesa computer. "Five-thirty."

"By the time we load the canoe it'll be light enough to read the
river."

Kid began to look for his trombone. "I don't see it."

"What are you talking about?" Molly asked, as she stood up
with a blanket wrapped around her shoulders.

"My trombone . . . of course."

"Oh . . . ," she said, as she looked toward her house. "I forgot
about it." She pulled out a pair of clean panties from her bag. "It's
at my place."

"We'll need it, Molly."

"Why?" She dropped the blanket and slipped on her cotton
underwear.

"Because we're going to Paris."

"Paris?" She pulled on a pair of shorts. "Paris doesn't exist."

"Molly, I'll explain later, but I've got to have my trombone."

"Can't you use the shakuhachi?" She slipped on a cotton
sweater, and started brushing her hair. "We don't need a circus,

Mister Monday.''

Kid grabbed her hand and started leading her down the stairs. The light had not reached the lower part of the Shoin. "We've got to get it now, Molly.'' He stopped at the first landing, and touched her face. "Molly . . . I'm sorry that I woke you up so suddenly.'' He kissed her nose. 'I'll explain everything later.''

"That's what I should be saying to you.'' There was a series of explosions at the upper end of Wandering Foot. "Oh no, they're dropping mortars into the staging area.'' She started running down the stairs. "You wait here, Kid, I'll get the trombone.''

He started following her. "No . . . we can't split up.''

Molly disappeared through the trees. Kid, not knowing the trail, was immediately lost in vegetation. "Damn it!'' He stumbled onto the river. Long fingers of mist and fog had settled over the water. A doe and fawn were grazing on the bank. An owl was making her last flight up river. Beyond, one of the sozus whomped in punctuation to the owl's wings. "Damn it Molly, where'd you go?''

Within minutes, Molly was back at her house. She ran into the zashiki, lifted up a section of tatami, and opened a small trap door. Kid's trombone was under a stack of old mats. She grabbed the handle and pulled it out. "You'd better make some sweet music with this,'' she said out loud. Five more explosions. Molly could hear the soldiers running along the path. "What timing.'' She looked around the main room. "I'll be back,'' she said, as she touched one of the bamboo uprights. "Someday.'' She opened the fusuma and stepped onto the veranda. Four guards ran noisily past the gate as they headed toward the main villa. A mortar dropped into one of the reflecting pools which sent water and koi shooting sixty feet into the air. "Holy shit,'' she yelled, as she ran through the garden. "Kid,'' she said to herself, "don't leave the Shoin.'' Without looking, she opened the gate and was suddenly stopped by General Liberty.

"Good morning, Molly,'' May said, as she looked at the trombone. "Going somewhere?''

"Oh . . . ,'' Molly replied, as she held the trombone in front of her. "I was . . . going to the staging area.''

"With Kid's trombone?'' Molly looked around the garden. "Where is he?''

"I don't know.''

"I think you're lying, Molly Rose.''

"I'm not . . .''

"Good, then you can come with me." May held the gate open.

"I'll ah . . . I forgot . . ."

"That's all right, Molly. Whatever it is you won't be needing it." She unholstered her pistol. "I think you can tell us where Kid is."

"I'm right here," Kid said, as he stepped out from behind an Ibuki tree.

May spun around. "Ahhh . . . the wizard." She pointed a nickel plated .38 magnum at his chest. Kid took one step toward her. "Don't move!" she shouted.

Kid raised his hands. "Come on, May . . ."

"Where's Coyote and Ava?" she demanded.

"I don't know."

"Bullshit." She rapidly pointed the weapon up the trail. "That way . . ."

"Listen," Kid said, "I can erase all of this." He pointed to the rim. "The men's army, their weapons . . ."

"You're talking bullshit, Monday. You told me you'd bring back those kids and all you did was try and run off with Molly."

"I really can, May." Kid was backing up the trail with the idea that May would forget about Molly. "This war could be history."

"How do I know you wouldn't do that to us?" She followed him up the trail. Kid was smiling.

"Because I have a great love for Wandering Foot."

"That's hard to believe, Kid."

"Give me a chance . . ."

"I'm taking you to the front, Mister Hot Shot."

Kid stopped backing up. "I only want Molly safe on the Fifth Mesa."

"Don't move!" May pushed out the pistol.

Kid stopped. "That's all I want."

May, losing eye contact with Molly, concentrated on Kid. She watched his eyes. The weapon quivered. "You're coming with me."

Kid watched Molly slip behind an azalea hedge. He stepped back. "I'll do anything to end this war."

"That's exactly what I have in mind, Kid."

"Okay." He smiled. Another barrage of mortar shells hit one of the ammo dumps. May spun toward the noise.

"God damn it!" she shouted.

Kid stopped. "If I'm going to help you, I think we'd better get going."

May, getting nervous, turned to find Molly as she tried to keep her eyes on Kid. "Where . . ."

"I'm right here," Molly said, as she stepped out from the hedge and whacked May over the head with the trombone case.

"Molly!" Kid shouted, "good thinking." He ran over to make sure May was unconscious. "Great job." He kicked the pistol into the pond. Molly was leaning over the case.

"I was so frightened."

"You really walloped her," he said, as he knelt down and felt May's pulse. "She's off to dreamland."

"I hated it, Kid, I hated it."

Kid slipped the case out from Molly's grip and held her in his arms. "It's okay."

"She'll be okay?" Her legs started to shake.

"Unfortunately . . . yes." He looked around to make certain no other soldiers were around. "Come on, let's get out of here."

Molly knelt down and touched May's face. "I'm sorry."

Kid walked away. "She was probably going to shoot us," he said inaudibly.

Molly picked an azalea and put it in May's hand. "I hope you . . . ah . . . win."

"Molly, she's not dead," he remarked to himself. "As soon as she comes to she'll send a whole herd of soldiers after us." He touched Molly's arm. "We should get out of here."

Molly stood up and stared into Kid's eyes. "I've never hurt anyone in my life."

"It's okay, Molly, even The Great Mother spanks her children." He laughed and touched Molly's cheek. "Maybe we should have invited May to go with us to Paris."

Molly jumped. "What?"

He took her hand and turned toward the river. "I was only joking."

Molly was walking backwards. "Paris is not for her, anyway."

"How about Beirut, 1987," Kid answered.

"That's cruel."

"That, unfortunately, is May's consciousness. Along with all of them who need to keep fighting." A bomb hit the main villa. They grabbed each other's hands and jumped over a yew tree that had been knocked down. "All of the mesas are out there, Molly, all of them."

Spider Woman knocked on the front door of The Great Mother's chalet, and looked back at the thunderheads building up over the village. She faced the clouds as if she were saying a prayer. The light was a wash of colors captured in pastels of shape. Raindrops skidded on the stone path and shattered into mist. Spider Woman heard a noise and stepped toward the door.

Mona, in the middle of changing her clothes, came running out of the bedroom. "Come in," she said, as she started looking for her shoes. Spider Woman slowly opened the door and peeked inside.

The Great Mother was dressed in a silk herringbone jacket over a silk batiste tuxedo shirt and charmeuse salon pants. "Are you leaving?" she asked, as she timidly stepped through the doorway.

"Not yet," Mona answered. "Please come in." A small fire was burning and the room smelled of pinyon pine and expensive perfume. "The Whoa Man and I are going up to the Seventh Mesa to find out why the Holy Highs have disappeared." She opened up a closet.

Spider Woman sat near the fire. "It's starting to rain." She held out her hands to warm them. "You look lovely."

Mona found the shoes at the bottom of the closet. "Thanks," she replied, as she put them on. "I've lost so much weight that there's hardly anything I can wear. Spider Woman watched in admiration as Mona put on a pair of gold earrings. "However, my feet are still the same size, or perhaps even larger." She walked over to the mirror and straightened her jacket. "How are you?" she asked.

"Fine."

"I had a good time this morning with the children." She turned around. "I was so surprised."

"They enjoyed your company," Spider Woman replied.

"I've been such a crab lately." She walked over to where Spider Woman was seated. "Maybe I'm finally going through menopause, but if that's true, I must be getting it from the entire female species." She touched her chest.

"It must be the moon," Spider Woman answered, "or, because it's gone."

"That's what I keep thinking." Mona walked around the room. Several of Spider Woman's weavings were hanging on the walls. "I'm worried about Kid, The Whoa Man can't seem to find a solu-

106

tion for creating another moon and The Cowboy Buddha is going bananas over the missing Hall of Famers." She rubbed the polished pine bannister that led to the loft.

A log crackled and then a pocket of pitch exploded. Spider Woman jumped as the sparks hit the screen. For over a minute she considered what she wanted to tell Mona. Finally, she looked at The Great Mother. "Tuesday and Ava are on their way to the Fifth Mesa."

"When?" Mona asked.

"Soon." Spider Woman took The Great Mother's hand. "They're coming by way of Morning Glory Pool."

Mona stood up, went over to the fire and poked at a log that had fallen off the grate. "You can still communicate like that?" The Great Mother asked.

Spider Woman picked up a piece of firewood and smelled it. It's the old way, she thought to herself. Once, all of the Holy People could communicate like that. Now, she was the only one. "I guess so," she replied.

"You saw them at the pool?" Mona turned to look at Spider Woman.

"Yes . . ."

Mona went over to the sink and washed her hands. "I . . . ah . . ."

"Would you like for me to meet them?"

Mona walked over to the mirror and began to brush her hair. "No . . . I . . ." She turned toward Spider Woman. "I haven't seen Tuesday in ten years." She put down the brush. "Honestly, Spider Woman, right now I feel somewhat intimidated." She tapped the brush in her palm. "That sounds strange, doesn't it? He was always so overwhelming to me, and Kid was just the opposite. He always needed more of whatever it was and Kid was happy with less." She leaned against the couch. "He's lucky that he has the Fifth Mesa to come back to."

"Yes, that's true," Spider Woman answered. She wanted to say more. About how fortunate it was that Tuesday was still alive, and that they were able to escape. But, she held off. "Everything needs to be rebalanced," she finally answered. She moved over to the hand carved window seat, sat down and closed her eyes as if to signal that she had settled the matter. Everybody will adjust.

Mona stepped closer to Spider Woman. "But, don't you see, I blew up the moon, and it was like I had blown up my own body." She raised her arms and made a soft imploding noise. "Sky high."

Spider Woman felt so warm and secure wrapped in the bay window. She also felt like going to sleep. The Great Mother couldn't exonerate herself from blowing up the moon and it looked like she was going to keep it until it defeated her. She didn't know what she could do to help. She would have to work on that. She opened her eyes and watched a small herd of deer graze casually in the garden. "Even if your experiment had worked, Mona, it would have only lasted a short time. Those who want to find true peace only have to make their way to the Fifth Mesa."

Mona wiped a tear off her cheek. "Oh, I so wanted the Third Mesa to be at peace, Spider Woman." She clenched her hands into fists. "I really believed that the women would never get involved down there. That they wouldn't try to duplicate the male consciousness. I just couldn't stand it any longer. I had to try." She clapped her hands and shook her head. "And look what happened."

"Only because you reacted in the male way."

A rainbow suddenly appeared inside the window. Spider Woman was bathed in colors. Mona gasped, "Don't move, Spider Woman, I want to take a picture of you just like that. It's magnificent."

Spider Woman was smiling as she felt her body slowing being dissolved by the light. "Mona," she said quietly, "don't take a photograph. Just come here and sit with me." She opened her eyes and held out her hand. "Please . . ."

Mona stopped. It would be nice, she thought, just to sit for awhile. Curl up like Spider Woman and float inside that wonderful light. For just a second she thought about her biography and what a great photograph it would make. Especially on the day she heard that her son was returning. She moved toward the bedroom. Spider Woman turned and held out her hand. Slowly, she removed her shoes and slipped into the seat. The rainbow wrapped itself around her body. "Oh . . . it's so warm."

Spider Woman was breathing very slowly. Again, her eyes were closed. "Ahhhh . . . this is peace." She laughed, and opened her eyes. "Step number one, Mona. Find a warm, soft spot and curl yourself up." She took Mona's hand. "Step two. Don't swing at anything that comes at you at the speed of light." She opened one eye. "And . . . step three . . ."

Mona was watching the light move around Spider Woman's body. "And . . . ?"

A smile seemed to come out of the rainbow that covered the

weaver's face. "And if you do swing, make certain that you're able to catch it."

*   *   .*   *   *

Molly flipped over the canoe and slipped it into the water. "Okay, Kid," she said, as she secured the stern, "tell me what's going on in that three-ring brain of yours."

Kid was resting on his haunches. "Well, after we . . . ah . . . you know . . . ah . . . made love . . ."

"Yes, I remember that we did . . . ," she reached over and touched his hand, "make love." She knelt down and started filling a waterproof bag with some of their belongings. There were three explosions near the hot springs. "We'd better get going."

"Wait," Kid answered. "After you fell asleep I was thinking how wonderful it would be if we could just get to Paris . . ."

"Kid, I thought you were joking. Paris is gone."

"Not now, Molly . . . but back at the end of World War One when . . ." Five more shells, falling near Molly's house, exploded.

"Kid, you'll have to tell me later."

Kid quickly put away his trombone and grabbed a life jacket as Molly strapped the waterproof bag into the canoe. "We'll just skip around through time where there are no wars."

"You'd better do it before we get to Double Lightning Falls," Molly shouted, as she untied the stern's painter. "Take the bow," she yelled.

Kid looked over at Molly. "You any good?"

"I canoed the Upper Canyon one time." She stabilized the canoe. "Jump in . . ." Kid stuffed his trombone under the middle thwart, and cautiously eased himself into the bow. Rubbed sponges had been glued onto the inner hull as knee guards. He knelt down in front of the bow seat and held onto the dock. "Okay . . ."

Molly put on her jacket and snapped the catches. "How good are you?"

Kid looked back. "I'm a fast learner."

"Holy shit," Molly replied. She reached over to the starboard gunwhale and pushed off. She slid gracefully in as the canoe cleared the dock. "Paddle from the starboard," she yelled.

A mortar shell hit thirty feet above them. The canoe slipped underneath an overhanging mountain cherry tree.

Molly dug her paddle into the fast moving water. "Go, go,

109

go . . ." The river was at maximum flow from the spring runoff. As the water swept them into the deep canyon the Shoin received a direct hit. Molly and Kid, in between strokes, looked back to see Coyote's old hideout disappear. "The sandpainting," she said, mostly to herself.

Kid corrected the bow from being shoved sideways by the stiff current. "I saw them get away," he shouted, as he turned back. "I saw them leave."

Molly looked puzzled as she dug into the water. "What . . . ?"

"Your Holy High buddies," he yelled. "Buddha Shooting Way and the gang."

"Yeah . . . sure . . . ," she answered. "Watch that rock," she yelled. "Pay attention . . ."

"Okay, okay," he replied. "He quickly glanced back at the Shoin. "You'll see, Molly," he said to himself. "You're going to be really surprised one of these days, really surprised." He executed a draw stroke which pulled the canoe around a large boulder.

"Lookin' good," Molly shouted above the river noise, "so far we're lookin' good."

"I always have," Kid said to himself as he turned his wizard's cap backwards. "Let's just hope this river behaves the same way." He looked back to make certain his trombone was securely tied in. Lovingly, he patted the case.

Cutting up the back way to Mesa Five, Coyote, with Ava in the lead, suddenly realized that he was feeling better. The pain in his leg had **13** diminished, and he didn't feel so exhausted. "Mesa Five," he said, "the Holy People's chicken soup." It also made him think about one of his exit lines to them. "It's boring in Paradise with your quantum updrafts of supreme well being."

He stopped and looked back on his father's ancestral home. Pleistocene air and paleozoic footholds into the future of Wandering Foot. He watched it being blown sky high. A shiver ran up his spine. He had to let it all go. Where was the blame?

He didn't know and didn't care.

He was almost happy with the thoughts of leaving it all behind. The lust. He laughed, and stood his ground as he felt his body being lassoed inside a quivering of health.

Tonight, he only had to make love with his mind.

He didn't even know if he could do that.

Hopefully, it would return, he thought.

He looked up at Ava. Three easy pitches away she was standing on a rock near a stand of quaking aspens. The leaves were chattering like Tibetan monks playing enlightenment tapes. There seemed to be no end to Ava's long legs as they vanished beyond the point where she rose out of the clouds. She had stripped down to shorts and a loose, open shirt. Thirteen pitches below, and one more to go.

Coyote pushed himself away from the rock and shoved off. Looking up, he watched her remove her shirt.

Ava was waiting at a small waterfall where the water dropped into a rock cavern surrounded by a cushion of grass and wild flowers. Columns of red sandstone bolted up from the banks of the pool. Two bald eagles, riding an updraft, hovered like guardians.

Below, Coyote watched her slip out of her shorts. Bracelets of gold rode up her arms like spiritual victories. She stepped into the water as if it were a mouth to feed and care for—cupping water, capturing reflections, and bringing food. She played in the cool water and waited.

*   *   *   *   *

"Tell me about the rapids," Kid yelled. They had come into an eddy where the water was being backed up by large rocks that pinched the flow. The light was layered by the rapidly changing morning.

Molly, resting her paddle on the rear thwart, lifted herself up and studied the river. "Okay," she said, as she back paddled to kick the canoe sideways so she wouldn't have to talk to the back of Kid's head. "The first rapid is a narrow channel that would be a disaster for us, but, over to the right is a little chute which we'll take. After that, there is a monster of a rock garden followed by some high rollers. So, to avoid these, we'll sneak along the bank. I'll keep the stern against the shore as close as possible and you'll have to keep the bow out at a forty-five degree angle so that the current holds us along the edge. After that, we go over to the left. There are five large rocks we've got to slalom through." She paused, and wiped a strand of wet hair out of her eyes. "That will be a gas, but get ready for the big mother."

Kid kept dipping his paddle into the water to hold the canoe in place. "How big?"

Molly held out both arms. "If there was any land we'd portage it."

112

"One big rodeo?" Kid asked.

Molly nodded. "After we go through the second set of rapids we'll head for the middle of the river and line up to take the only channel available. There's a four foot falls with a mother of a keeper hole at the bottom, so after we jump the falls start paddling like a crazy man." She heard something above her, but when she looked up all she could see was the newly awakened sky.

Kid, perched on the seat, dropped down on his knees to lower the center of gravity. Molly swung the canoe around and started paddling toward the narrow channel. The riverbed was taking most of the water off to the left—leaving only a small amount for the right channel. They scooted through the chute as if they were on a roller coaster. They yelled and shouted, and at one point the rock walls were so close they could have reached out and touched both sides.

"Now . . . right ferry, Kid," Molly shouted.

Kid reached across the bow to draw his end out into the main current as Molly backpaddled and pried the stern to keep it as close to the bank as she could. Snuggled against the shore, they were able to avoid the rocks and white water passing through the rock garden.

"Now," Molly shouted, when they cleared the garden, "head to the opposite bank."

Kid kicked the bow over with a crossdraw. Once they had the canoe lined up for a left ferry they quickly floated to the far bank. Molly studied the rocks and the high water from the run-off. She called out the next sequence—yelling for Kid to backpaddle—wanting to go in as slowly as possible. She didn't want to hot dog it with the water so high. They teased around the first rock, cut over to the right, and slipped past the second one. They were in a dance, moving as one, thinking the same patterns, keeping the canoe in control when they came up on a submerged rock. They hit it broadside, ran up and spun downriver. Molly grabbed the upriver gunwale to keep the water from swamping the canoe.

"Whoa there!" she shouted. "Draw!" she yelled. She straightened out the stern, dug into the water and the canoe dropped over the rock and into a large hole which blasted Kid with spray.

Once they had cleared the hole, he propped his paddle on the gunwales and wiped his eyes. "Woooooweeeeeee," he yelled, "for a second I thought we were just going to keep on spinning."

"Hey, we did good," Molly shouted, as she bailed out the water with a large bamboo bucket.

"Smooth as silk changing into pantyhose," Kid yelled back. He lifted himself up to see the next set. "Is that the big one?"

"That's it."

"It doesn't look like much . . ."

"Dream on mad fool . . ." Molly made certain that all of their gear was still laced in. "After that, there's a small beach where we can land. I think it just might be time to catch that ride to Paris."

Kid reached back and patted his trombone. "I'll be ready." The canoe was moving into faster water. Kid wiped his brow and got down as low as he could. There were two fifty-foot moss covered rocks before them. A layer of mist was chasing itself in curlicues on the water's surface with a rainbow slipping in between the rocks. Molly was talking to Kid about how they had to keep the canoe exactly between the rocks.

"Easy . . . easy . . . ," Molly kept saying over and over again, "just backpaddle . . . easy . . . line her up . . . stay right in the middle and think the happiest thoughts you can possibly imagine. This is no time to be timid. Or frightened. We can swear, call the river dirty names just to let it know Molly and Kid are coming through. Scum bag, poop-head, double douche bag, dildo face, alligator vomit, and then slip in a gentle prayer just to fake it out. But don't . . . don't ever let the river know you're afraid. Respectful, but never afraid. That's right . . . easy . . . and . . . we're moving into the fast water now . . . and . . . we're lined up . . . and . . . and . . . now!" Molly leaned down and jammed her paddle into the water. "Go, Go, Go, Go, Go . . ."

Kid heard the command and felt the surge as he ripped his paddle into the water. Suddenly, his entire being was filled with the noise from the river as it was forced between the two enormous rocks.

"Dig, Dig, Dig, Dig . . . ," he heard Molly shout.

They hit the chute—sliding into wet thunder—riding out Mesa Five's spring thaw, and within seconds they were sailing over the edge of the falls. Kid was looking into the hole as the water boiled below. He missed one stroke as they dropped onto the outer edge of the hole. He heard Molly shout as he leaned out as far as possible for his next stroke. His paddle struck a rock and it was ripped out of his hands and thrown twenty feet into the air. The canoe, having been filled with too much water when it went over the falls,

114

was sucked back in.

Kid rolled out when the canoe flipped back. He tried to grab Molly, but all he got was an image of her taking in one last breath of air as she rode the canoe down. He was kicked out and pushed onto a large, flat rock. He spun around, slipped and finally lifted himself up to where he could see the outer edge of the hole.

"Molly!" he screamed.

"Molly, for God's sake don't . . . "

The bottom fell out of his soul because he knew that the water's hydraulics could keep her down there until she drowned. He ripped off his life jacket and jumped into the water. Instantly, he was swept downstream. He managed to flip onto his back so he could fend off the rocks with his feet.

"Molly . . . !"

His feet touched the bank. Without thinking, he ran upstream, climbed over an outcropping of boulders, scaled the fifty foot rock on the right side of the channel, jumped into the water above the falls and rode it down into the hole.

As he dropped in head first the canoe came shooting past him. He saw a face and then he was being tumbled around like a rag doll. Still, he managed to keep his eyes open as he looked for Molly. He wasn't going to let it happen. No way. He was a Holy Person. Right? Didn't these river demons understand that?

Molly, who had stayed with the canoe, was floating on top and sucking in deep breaths of air. She had some memory of Kid. What was it? Jumping in as she was being catapulted out? Did he go back in? No . . . she must be hallucinating. The water was so calm now. So peaceful and calm. She paddled in the eddy.

Over and over again Kid was being tumbled.

Still, he wasn't giving in. But, he realized that he would have to save his own life. He couldn't believe it had come to that. He jammed his knee against something soft. He reached back and hung on. Damn! What was it? Molly's body?

Molly was certain she had seen Kid clear the hole when they went in but where was he now? She beached the canoe and found his jacket wrapped around a rock.

"Kid . . . !"

She grabbed it and waded back in. "Kid!" Frantically, she looked up and down the river. "Oh no . . . "

Kid's mind screamed for Molly.

115

He pulled at the body until it broke free of the rocks. Centrifugally, they were pushed to the outer edge of the hole as he wrapped his arms around it and pressed his face into its softness.

Five times they were whipped around until they were eventually rejected. Like a new life demanding oxygen, he thrust his head up and sucked in huge amounts of air. Molly, stumbling through the water, tried to grab his hand. Twice she fell. The current kept pushing her back into the eddy.

"Kid . . . !"

Molly was washed in sunlight. He reached out his hand to this stranger.

"Grab on . . . damnit!"

"Where did she come from?"

They were at the line between the eddy and the next rush of water to Double Lightning Falls. He stretched out his hand. She plunged in and found his hand. Their fingertips curled into flesh.

"Paddle!" she screamed.

"Grab that rock!"

"Let go of the trombone . . . "

"No . . . she's still alive."

"You're crazy . . . " Miraculously, she was able to find a knob on the rock and a footing in the sand. Kid lunged and grabbed her forearm. "You're a fool . . . Kid."

"I'm in love . . . "

"Why'd you go back in?"

"For Molly . . . "

"Bullshit . . . "

Suddenly, Kid realized that it was his trombone he was holding. "I thought it was you." He let it go.

"Right." She grabbed the case as she pulled him in.

"Molly . . . is this you?" He stumbled and fell on top of her.

The sky had turned a pale magenta that spilled across the canyon. An osprey, on its territorial patrol, floated overhead. Two salmon jumped out of the calm back water as if to laugh at the fish eagle. The walls had opened up. There was a softness and width—a breath where something could land, nourish itself and grow. The wild flowers were tall and abundant, and two deer drank at the river's edge.

Molly and Kid were at the edge of the Fourth Mesa. It was lush and addictive. Invisible spirits seemed to be everywhere.

Molly joked about Kid going back in for Cheyenne Rose.

They laid in the grass until they were dry and then they made love.

Rolling through the flowers

remembering the hole where they had been captured as they clawed, grasped and screamed—attacking each other like animals— opening up into primal wounds of their expected loss.

Anger slowly gave way to lust which gradually released itself into love which fell helplessly through layers of consciousness until they found themselves dissolved in pollen.

They floated inside the backwater of their containment

All morning within that vast pool of first love where the heart beat was like the bam boom pipe calling their names

The rocks above them

like smiling gargoyles—

hovered as guardians.

*　　*　　*　　*　　*

Spider Woman and Mona were walking slowly to Morning Glory Pool. The children, who at the last moment had been yanked out of the computer room by The Great Mother, were scattered in every direction. The sun had come out, and only a few tufts of whiskered clouds remained. The air was pungent with the ripe scents of juniper and pine, and with each step hundreds of iridescent droplets showered the tall grasses. Beyond, the mountains seemed so much higher as if the short cloudburst had flattened the scenery against the long cordillera range.

Off in the distance, sheep bells punctuated the children's joyous laughter. Two mating falcons dove into the scene's consciousness— shooting straight up from ten feet off the ground.

The Great Mother sighed as she held on to Spider Woman's arm. "It feels so good to be here with you and the children."

Two of them ran past. "Can't catch me . . ."

"Neener, neener, neener."

Shoes had been removed and left with the women.

"Hey . . . that's hot man."

"Wow, the Fifth Mesa is really cool."

"We should start making extinct species like Kid and Coyote did.'

"Yeah, and bring back the dinosaurs."

117

"The Whoa Man is working on a new project called The Yap of the Whoa."

Spider Woman tugged at Mona's arm. "Don't they sound wonderful?" The Great Mother smiled. "I'm surprised that you asked them to come along."

The Great Mother stopped. "It just happened that way when I was on my way to meet you. As I passed the computer center there they were just hanging out without supervision, and I could see that something had to be done."

"It would be nice if we started a school for them."

Mona picked up a rubber ball that had rolled near her feet, and threw it to Lisa. "I agree." "Perhaps Ava and Tuesday would like to run it."

The Gyre falcons returned in an acrobatic ballet of spring passion. Two feathers broke loose and came floating down the meandering meadow.

"Hey LaMar, did you see that?"

"Yeah man . . ."

"Leonardo said he would help me build a helicopter."

"Are we really going to meet Tuesday Coyote?"

"Ava Matisse was the greatest women's fighter they ever had."

"You're it . . ."

Jamal came running back from the cliff that overlooked Morning Glory Pool. "Hey you guys, it's right over there." He slid to a stop. "I could see all the way to the bottom."

"There's no bottom, dummy," Heidi challenged.

Mona started running toward the edge. "Did you see them?" she asked Jamal.

"No . . ."

All of the children gathered around The Great Mother and Spider Woman. "Where are they?"

The falcons, descending in spirals, landed in separate trees near the pool.

"There they are," Rosie said, "I can see them by the pool."

"Oh, she's pretty."

The two parties were separated by a stand of Quaking aspens—the white bark spotted like Appaloosa horses. Mona pulled Lisa against her as she searched for her son.

"Look, they're coming up the trail."

Coyote, dressed in his brightly colored shirt, walked as if he had

118

lost his limp. Ava seemed to glide up the trail. They were holding hands. The Great Mother clutched her breast when she saw them. "There he is." She reached for more children.

"Hey Coyote," the youngest boy shouted.

Tuesday took off his hat and waved. "Yo . . ."

Spider Woman moved behind Mona as if she wanted to gently nudge her down the trail. She took Rosie's hand. "Go on . . . Rosie . . . go meet them."

Rosie started and then turned back. "Come on you guys, they won't hurt you."

The Great Mother was still hanging on to Lisa who was tugging to get away. "Let me go," she said . . . , "please."

Mona released her grasp as the young girl's momentum pulled The Great Mother forward.

"The last one down the trail is a rotten egg."

Some of the children, released by the trail's grade, began to run.

The scene fluttered within the cockeyed angle of the aspen leaves, the light bouncing off the pool, the gaiety of voices. Mona felt so happy that she could hardly breathe, and it seemed to her that she had lived that moment for a thousand or two years. Still, it was a hard sting and also a blessed one to welcome the warriors. The battle was over and only the love of life would ever heal the wounds. At that moment she understood what she had been, and it was like all of the children had sprung out of her body. She laughed and started to run with them. It was all right now. In fact, she could probably even beat them. Lisa tripped over a rock and she grabbed the young girl's arm quickly. The Great Mother lifted her onto her shoulders. The children already had the visitors surrounded—arms curled around soft forgiving bodies—faces squashed into warmth. Coyote tried to find her, but all he saw were ancient faces dancing among the trees. Every ancestor—ghost seeds dancing molecules in the spheres—outer and inner space. Trading off and leaving no tracks.

Their dark eyes pulled in the distance until they were touching each other's place where conception was ordained. A smile broke open and then laughter.

A fire was burning in front of the cave that Molly and Kid had used for their temporary home. Their clothes were laid out to dry, and **14** Kid was cooking a salmon that he had cradled inside a grill made from woven green willows. Molly walked over to the fire, squatted down and offered him a handful of wild strawberries. Their bodies were tanned, and the graceful lines of their youth carried an easy androgyny between them.

"Our first morning of freedom," Molly said, as she tasted the fish. She stuck a strawberry into his mouth as she looked wistfully upriver.

Kid's green eyes sparkled as he crinkled up his freckled nose. He brushed a lock of his blond hair and closed his eyes. "Man like woman who feed him wild strawberries."

"Woman much more fulfilled eating out in expensive restaurants."

"Ugh . . . no restaurants . . ."

"Then man hire cook," Molly answered. Again, she looked toward Wandering Foot.

Kid jumped up. "In restaurants man cannot always eat wild strawberries out of woman's

121

navel. Or, make secret love calls to the fish." He pretended to stomp around the fire. "No good . . ."

Molly held a strawberry over each nipple. "You like, monsieur?"

Kid leaped onto a large rock and beat his chest. "I . . . great wild man called The Kundalini Crusher . . . like."

Molly picked up Kid's trombone case and began to unsnap the locks. "I think, Monsieur Crusher, that it's time for a well earned vacation." Vacantly, she looked into the open case. "Poor old Wandering Foot."

Kid jumped down. "You're absolutely right because I feel like I've been here since the Pleistocene humped Genesis." He danced around her and easily lifted his trombone from her hands. "Ahhh . . . baby," he murmured, as he kissed its rose gold bell. He ran into the field of flowers. A large juniper was growing inside an outcropping of sandstone. "Perhaps we should build a little cafe right here."

"Sure," Molly answered, as she slowly followed Kid into the meadow. "A bed and breakfast for all of those Third Mesa people." She plucked a long blade of grass and spun the stem. "Already, I miss them, Kid, even General May."

Kid finally noticed her mood change. He ran over and touched her face. "Hey . . . I'm sorry."

She leaned against his chest. "Me too."

He kissed her hair and wrapped his arms around her shoulders. His trombone reflected her slender body in stretched and widened shapes. "I think it's time that we take our trip to Paris." Again, he kissed her. "Don't you?"

Molly kissed his chest. Her eyes, canted in a customized rake of polished angles, stared into his shoulder. Kid touched her chin. Slowly, she lifted her head. "I'm ready."

Kid gently guided her over to the large rock. "Give me the orchestration," he said, as he ran his hand softly along her graceful body.

Molly sighed, and looked at the low stratocumulus clouds that were drifting over the rolling canyon walls. "Okay . . . it's 1919." She looked over at Kid. "Right?"

He pumped the slide. "Okay . . . 1919 it is. The war has just ended. No . . . wait a second. Let's go for the spring of 1920." He looked at her and shrugged.

Molly smiled. "All of the trees are in bloom . . ."

"The Paris Air Show is about to begin . . ."

"We have a little chateau near the river . . ."

"We have signed you up to fly a Sopwith Camel . . ."

I'm pregnant . . . but I haven't told you yet."

"With a brand new Hispano Suisa engine . . ."

"It will be the first of perhaps a thousand kids . . ."

"You have won five hundred thousand franks . . ."

"You have a little teaching job at the music conservatory . . ."

"We are extremely rich . . ."

"We are poor but extremely happy . . ."

Kid, with the sun shining through the hairs of his golden body, looked illuminated. He reached into his pack and pulled out the bottle of elixir. "I've always wanted to see that air show." He dumped the contents into the trombone. He rubbed the bell once more and ran the slide back and forth. "You'll be flying with all of the aces from World War One and they'll be Fokkers, Albatross D.V.'s, Spads, Bristols, and some older Sopwith Triplanes. That's for a start, Molly. They'll be zooming and streaking around, performing all kinds of dangerous acrobatics, and you, hot shot pilot that you're about to become, will be smack in the center of all of this wonderful peace-time craziness."

Molly picked up a long-stemmed oat grass and stuck it in her mouth. "We have this little French car, a wonderful cook because I'm such a lousy one that you insist she lives with us. Out of survival, of course." Molly sat down on the rock and stroked Kid's leg.

"And don't forget, Molly, that they didn't have parachutes in those days."

"I want to have a wicker perambulator, and we'll put up peaches and pears, apricots, beans, tomatoes . . . all from our garden, and I'll learn French, and start teaching classes based on the Gandhi Dancer."

Kid slipped the slide back and forth. "My brother and Ava will join us . . ."

"And we'll make love twice a day for five hundred years . . ."

"They'll amaze everyone with their skydiving tricks."

"As soon as we earn enough money from our hard work we'll buy a little farm in the south of France where we'll spend our winters . . ."

"This is going to be so hot . . ."

"Oh Kid, I'm so happy." She grabbed Kid around the neck. "Let's do it."

"All right," he shouted, as he returned her kiss. "Goodbye all you mesas . . . we're goin' back to the land of French kisses and brie, honeymoons and square boxed touring cars." He got down on one knee to steady his trombone, and then he placed the image that he had so expertly choreographed securely in his mind. He blew Molly a good luck kiss. "This is it . . ."

"Wait . . . !" Molly shouted, as she became aware of what Kid had said, "What's this about a Sopwith?" She tried to grab Cheyenne Rose.

Kid spun out of her way, twirled three times, and, as he raised his trombone to the sky, he shot out a bubble that instantly became the greatest peace time celebration that Europe had seen in over six years.

For Ava's and Coyote's homecoming all of the exercise machines were stored in the community center's basement. A temporary bar was made from saw horses and old doors, flowers were flown in from all of the upper mesas, and April Fools, the main organizer and chef for the occasion, had made up finger foods that resembled pastels tucked in and around folds of baby knees. Ava and Coyote arrived early so they would have a chance to talk with The Whoa Man before the guests arrived. They found him hunkered under bushy eyebrows at the bar. Ava had changed into a clean powder blue jumpsuit and sandals. Coyote, in jeans, satin shirt, red headband, was wrapped inside the spirit of his Third Mesa father as he tried to make the adjustments that were necessary to live on the Fifth Mesa.

The Whoa Man tapped his head after he had given both of them a limp handshake. "Your brother and Molly are in Paris, France."

Ava glanced over at Coyote. "What . . . ?" Coyote squinted as he cocked his head.

The Whoa Man laughed and touched Ava's

forearm. "I'm the only one who knows."

Coyote took a deep breath and slowly released it. "I was beginning to wonder what had happened to them." He looked around for his mother.

"Those rats," Ava said dramatically, "but what a great idea. I wonder if there's any way . . ." She paused and turned to her husband. "Do you think we could get there?" She leaned against his head. "I mean . . . a mother-in-law is still a . . ."

"Right . . . ," Coyote replied. "I hear you." During breakfast, Mona had talked them about their future plans, and when he mumbled something about a long rest, she asked him if he would put a new roof on her chalet. He turned toward The Whoa Man. "Can you get them on your computer?"

The Whoa Man made some adjustments on his wrist computer and then held out his arm. "There they are roaring through the Twenties . . . folks."

Ava grabbed his wrist. "Look . . . that's got to be the Bois de Boulogne because there's the racecourse at Longchamps . . . and see . . . Molly is climbing into some old airplane." She looked questioningly at Coyote, "I didn't know she could fly."

He shook his head. "That's a Sopwith Camel and there's Kid ready to prop the engine."

The Whoa Man tapped the computer. "Molly doesn't look very happy."

"Oh poop Coyote," Ava said, "I can almost smell the food and hear the music." She turned back toward the main doors. Heidi and Rosie arrived on Leonardo's arms. Spider Woman came in with LaMar and Jamal. They waved and headed for the food table. "We haven't been in Paris in years." She grabbed Coyote's arm. "Damn . . . that would be fun."

The Whoa Man turned off the monitor. "I'd sure like to be of some assistance . . ."

"Shit . . . !" Coyote shouted, as he jammed his fist against the palm of his other hand. "I can't even make love let alone get us to Paris." He grabbed a glass of champagne as it was being passed around by one of the younger girls. He clinked Ava's and The Whoa Man's glass. "I'm sure Kid and Molly are going to need some help." He glanced at Ava and nodded. "Right . . . ?"

Ava was shaking her head. "It's all so surreal, Tues, like I'm weightless and floating inside a cartoon of April Fools' mind and he's calling it The Nirvana Express and it's going so slow I can't jump off." She looked over at the food table that was sixty feet long and piled with over a hundred different kinds of finger foods. "I must be having Mesa Lag . . . or something like that."

Coyote was listening to Swiss Army Knife tell his Enlightenment Story at the grand piano. Cosmic Riddle and April Fools were seated on the stool. "What a blow hard," Coyote said, as he turned toward The Whoa Man. "You've got to help us."

The Whoa Man blew into his hands and rubbed them together. "I don't know, Tues . . . I couldn't even mathematically assist you with an old fashioned, Third Mesa erection."

"Hey brother," Coyote responded casually, "that wasn't your fault."

"Whoa Man," Ava said, "you invented Beyond Infinity, right?" She took a drink of champagne and stepped closer to the scientist. "Can't you go backwards and just leave us off . . . in Paris?"

One Hand Clapping strolled by and casually ran her hand across Coyote's butt. "Welcome back," she said, and continued on.

"Hey . . . I saw that." Ava shouted, as she stared at One Hand. "The next thing I know you'll be humping my husband with your mind. Right?"

Coyote turned to see what she was yelling about. "What's going on?"

"I'm defending my turf . . . that's what!" she answered.

"But everybody's giving each other mental orgasms all the time," he replied. "It's no big deal."

Ava kicked The Whoa Man playfully in the shins. "And you're responsible for that . . . right?" She grabbed Coyote's ear and kissed his cheek. "It's going to take me awhile to get used to mental orgasms that's for sure."

The Whoa Man was seriously trying to come up with an idea that would send Ava and Coyote to Paris. "I don't know . . . my last experiment blew up the moon." He shrugged, as Nuclear Spud was wheeled in by the Cowboy Buddha and Curve Ball. "Hey Nukie," he yelled, as he lifted his glass. He looked over at Ava. "If I could just figure out how to create another moon . . . I would be happy."

The Flying Findhorns came dancing across the garden. Coyote and Ava waved. "I wish I could help you out, Whoa Man," Coyote said, "but it'll be some time before I get my Fifth Mesa powers back."

"What about when you and Kid created those extinct species?" Ava asked. "Couldn't you use some of that sorcery?"

Coyote laughed, and kicked his boot against the saw horse. "Ahhh . . . that was mostly Kid's doing." He jammed his hands into his pockets. "We sure had some weird mojo back then."

"You could try," Ava challenged.

"I don't know, Ava," Coyote answered.

"Whoa Man," Ava said enthusiastically, "what about when you invented Fifth Mesa orgasms? Didn't you get a whole bunch of Holy People together to help out?"

Coyote looked over at The Whoa Man. "Yeah . . . what about it?"

The Whoa Man shook his head. "College pranks compared to this. Kid's the only one who can do what you're asking."

"It's worth a try," Coyote said.

The Whoa Man started rubbing his hands together just as Quarterback Sneak came out from under the piano and signalled a touchdown. Rodeo Tai Chi jumped on the Holy Man's back and started riding him through the garden. "That's right, that's right," The Whoa Man said, mostly to himself. He pulled out a notebook and started jotting down some numbers. "If we . . ."

Coyote shot up a thumb. "He's cooking, Ava . . . I know it."

Mona, arriving in with the rest of the children, stopped by on their way to the food table. She was wearing a sleeveless black silk chiffon dress covered with sequins and bugle beads. She touched Ava's hand. "The two of you look so serious," she said as she glanced over at The Whoa Man. "I know that look." She took her son's arm. "What's going on?"

"Well . . . ah . . . ah . . . ," Coyote stammered, as he wagged his head toward The Whoa Man, "you're sidekick here was trying to explain to us how he invented Mental Orgasms, and we thought that it just might be a gas if we had a little reenactment." He shrugged. "That's all . . ."

"Coyote wasn't around when that happened," Ava added, "and I, having spent my early life in art museums, and later on in the war, didn't hear about it until now."

Mona smiled, as she examined their eyes. "You should learn." Lisa, the youngest girl, was tugging at her dress. "Okay okay . . . I'm coming." The Great Mother touched her son's face. "I'm a little worried about Kid."

Coyote started to laugh as he thought about Molly and Kid living it up in Paris. "I think he's fine," he replied, "I wouldn't worry about him at all."

Mona kissed him on the cheek. "I hope you're right, son . . ." She took Lisa's hand as they walked over to the food table.

"All right," Tuesday said softly, as he grabbed a stool and sat down, "let's get this triple by-pass machine rolling!"

The Whoa Man pointed to his formula. "We'll have to wing it on what we've got right here in this room, but I'm certain she'll fly."

Ava and Coyote looked at his calculations. "Looks good to me," Ava answered. She leaned against Coyote's shoulder. "Right?"

"I'm ready . . ."

"See," The Whoa Man continued, "I've got One Hand Clapping, who seems to have the most powerful orgasmic ability on the Mesa, pitching a standard Sandy Koufax curve ball to Babe Ruth's Home Run Swing." He checked both of them to see if they were following his formula. "You got that?"

"Sounds good," they said in unison.

The Whoa Man turned his back to the rest of the Holy People and children. "Okay . . . so Ruth's Swing misses which creates enough energy inside Nuclear Spud's mini-reactor to push Porch Swing backwards, and when she gets up to . . . say . . . six hundred thousand r.p.m.'s per . . . that will create so much mass which in turn will start turning my memory and once I get back to the Twenties, Drop Kick will whack a good one right back to One Hand . . . and whammo . . . she's once again achieved supreme enlightenment and when all the smoke clears . . . you're out of here . . ."

"Wow!" Coyote shouted. "It's that simple?"

Ava grabbed her husband's mouth. "Not so loud."

The Whoa Man wiped his brow as he went through his procedure. He started speaking from the side of his mouth. "You go around the room and collect the Holy People we need, and I'll keep working on the formula." He tapped his pencil against the paper. "And make it look natural."

Nonchalantly, Ava and Coyote started mingling with the Holy People until they had informed everyone about the plan.

"You got it," One Hand Clapping said, as she kissed Ava on the cheek. "And give this to Kid when you see him, dear Coyote." She smiled, closed her eyes, and within seconds Coyote was spinning around in a circle. When he stopped, One Hand touched Ava's arm. "I hope that you'll be coming back here soon because it would be wonderful to have you here with us." She took Drop Kick's arm. "Imagine, a real Matisse living up here."

Ruth's Swing, Nuclear Spud, Curve Ball, Porch Swing and Drop Kick all thought it was a great idea and gathered around The Whoa Man. When he finally decided that he had his calculations perfected, he told all of the participants to make it look as if they were only recreating the orgasm routine. "That will keep everyone happy until blastoff time."

"Why don't you want Mona to know?" Curve Ball asked.

The Whoa Man put his finger over his mouth. "Since we blew up the moon together, she's made it very clear that I'm not to mess with any of your powers." Slowly, he started walking toward the French doors that led into the garden. "She hasn't gotten over the moon incident," he added.

Coyote and Ava followed the group.

The Cowboy Buddha, who was talking with Mona about the missing Holy Highs, noticed the group in the rose garden. "What's going on?" he asked.

Mona shrugged, "Oh . . . it looks like The Whoa Man is just talking about the good old days when he still had all of his incredible powers." She put her arm through his. "I don't think he's gotten over his part in blowing up the moon."

"And how about you?" The Cowboy Buddha asked.

Mona sighed and shook her head. "Oh . . . I'm still upset about it, naturally, but . . ."

Thermos, who was in charge of the computers for the evening, came running over and informed Mona and The Cowboy Buddha that Wandering Foot had just been destroyed.

"Everything?"

Thermos nodded. "As far as I can tell."

"What about Kid?" Mona asked.

"He and Molly got out by canoe, but we've lost them." Thermos shook his head.

"How could that be?" The Cowboy Buddha questioned.

"I'm not sure," Thermos replied, "but I think it has something to do with the disappearance of the Holy Highs from the Hall of Fame.

"Do you think they could be in cahoots?" the Holy Highs' agent asked.

Mona laughed. "Come on, Kid doesn't know how to be in . . . as you say . . . cahoots with anyone." She started toward the rose garden.

Lisa and Jamal ran over and joined her. "What are they doing out there?" the young man asked.

"Ladies and Gentlemen," The Whoa Man said, as he turned in a circle. "I would like to present a little skit in honor of Tuesday Coyote and Ava Matisse and their return to the Fifth Mesa. They were asking me about mental orgasms and so I offered to demonstrate, along with some of our esteemed colleagues, how it was discovered a few years ago. Which, as we all remember, eliminated a lot of useless hassles."

"Mind fuck, mind fuck, mind fuck . . . ," April Fools chanted as he jumped onto an outdoor table.

"Sssshhhhhhhh . . ."

"Therefore, with your cooperation, let's show Ava and Tuesday how it was accomplished." The Whoa Man clapped his hands and took his position. Ava and Coyote were standing between Drop Kick and One Hand Clapping.

"Is this how you guys blew up the moon?" Lisa asked The Great Mother.

"No . . . ," she answered, as she put her arms around her. "They're just playing around."

"Don't be nervous," Coyote said, as he took his wife's hand."

"Is this going to hurt?" Ava asked.

Coyote laughed. "At first it should feel something like a normal orgasm." He shrugged. "I think . . . and then I'm not sure what will happen."

"What?" Ava shouted, as she stepped out of position.

He grabbed her hand and pulled her back in place. "We'll just hit the pure orgasmic white light and then pass through Whiter-Than-White-Light and then whammo baby . . . we're out of here."

"It won't blow up?"

"Come on . . . you sound like a Victorian prude."

"I am, baby, when it comes down to messing with my body," Ava answered. "After I survived the war I don't want to be vaporized into everlasting tingles of holy come."

Coyote laughed, and kissed his wife's cheek. "I think One Hand is ready."

"The bitch . . ."

"Damn it Ava, she's only trying to help."

"Then wipe that eternal smile off your face when you look at her," Ava ordered. "Mental orgasms indeed."

Coyote shrugged. "Well . . . it's all we've got."

One Hand Clapping stepped into position, turned toward the audience and bowed. Then, she slowly pivoted so that she was facing Ruth's Home Run Swing.

"It's okay, baby, it's okay . . . ," Ruth's Swing said, trying to concentrate and keep One Hand calm. "Jus' get ol' Curve Ball in here." He swung his bat halfway and held it there as he remembered when The Great Mother had swung at the ball. "Jus' miss it, baby."

One Hand put the image she wanted into her head. It was in Paris in the Twenties and it was where she had first traveled after she had achieved her first enlightenment. The streets, the smells, the food, the artists all gathered together after the First World War. She got it all into her head before she started her windup. "Just one miss from Ruth," she said. "Just one easy miss." She stuck out her tongue just like she had seen so many pitchers do. Three times around, and then, with as much power as she could generate, she fired the curve ball at the plate. Ruth's Home Run Swing missed with such ferocity that it split Nuclear Spud's atoms which started up her generators that had been hooked up to Porch Swing and off she went—around and around—faster and faster until The Whoa Man engaged his brain which activated his reverse Beyond Infinity memory which began turning backwards from where Kid and Molly had been when they left the Third Mesa. The Nineties rolled past, the Eighties, the Seventies whirled around, the Sixties were gone in seconds, the Fifties. Smoke was pouring out The Whoa Man's ears, and some of the taller children started pouring champagne over his head. He was shaking, his eyes were twirling, but he stayed with it through the Forties, the Thirties, click, click, click, and it was thirty-five, thirty-four, thirty-three . . . clicking, clicking and everyone was cheering him on even though they couldn't understand why he was going back through time to duplicate his mental orgasm discovery, but what difference did it make because everyone seemed to be having such a good time. Click, click, click and it was Twenty–One and then December and then November and back through the months until it was June and then May thirty-first, thirtieth . . . and on down until he came to May Fifth which activated Drop Kick's Mental Orgasm which caused him to whack One Hand Clapping into full enlightenment which sent, as The Whoa Man had precisely calculated, Ava and Coyote on a one-way direct orgasmic white-light-flight to Paris-in-the-Twenties.

Stopping to rest near the Porte de Boulogne, Ava noticed a poster with May flying her Sopwith Camel. "Look at this, Coyote, Molly's already a big star."

16

Coyote checked his computer. "We're just in time." He pulled out the guide book they had purchased at the Eiffel Tower. "The air show is being held at the Longchamp Racecourse." He opened up the book that covered Bois de Boulogne. Suddenly they heard a lot of loud, happy screams, and then they noticed a group of people pointing toward the Seine. A large, twelve-part balloon was floating over the racecourse.

"That's gotta be Kid," Ava shouted.

"No one blows bubbles like that."

"Look at everyone head that way." She grabbed Coyote's hand. "Let's go."

They started to run through the entrance of the park, but Coyote had to stop because his leg was hurting him again. "I'll have to slow down." He put his arm around Ava's shoulders. "It was feeling so good up on Mesa Five."

"Maybe we should get you to a doctor."

"No way," Coyote answered, "I want to find Kid." A second bubble went floating into the air that looked like an overweight belly dancer. "Even when we were kids it was always easy to find my brother." Coyote took a step and winced.

"I can't wait to see him and Molly."

A third bubble went up and when the three of them came together they exploded into the celebration that Kid had always imagined a French air show to be: a carnival along the banks of the Seine, an outdoor circus near the Grande Cascade, food tent on the banks of the lakes that offered a variety of foods, wine tents and beer carts, vendors selling chestnuts, hurdy-gurdy machines, horse carts, dog shows, monkeys dressed in costumes, and the stadium inside the Longchamp racecourse was filled with people from all over Europe. The odor of food floated through the Bois de Boulogne as the musicians strolled through the crowds. Everyone in the stands was watching the air show that had just started, and the merchants were hoping for the best day of business since the signing of the Armistice.

An airplane flew over the Boulevard Anatole and banked toward the Auteuil Racecourse. "Holy Cow," Ava yelled, "that looked like Molly." She leaped into the air and waved. "Hey . . . !"

Coyote grabbed her hand and tried to run as fast as he could. "I don't care how much it hurts, let's find Kid." They ran as quickly as Coyote could possibly move until they came to the entrance on Route les Tribunes. "Ahhh . . . a wine tent," Coyote said, as he slowed down and licked his lips. "I could use a glass of wine the size of my boots."

Three bi-planes, flying in formation, zoomed over the stadium, and then another bubble floated in their wake. There was some writing on it which read, "Coyote Ugly."

Coyote laughed. "Did you see where it came from?"

"Yeah, over there," Ava said, pointing across the stadium. Coyote started to run but quickly stopped. "Easy there, Tues, your brother's not going anywhere." Coyote put his arm around Ava's shoulders. "What's this Coyote Ugly business?" she asked.

Coyote looked at his wife. "Oh . . . it's something our fathers always joked about."

"Well tell me . . ."

Coyote found an old pair of Vaurnet sunglasses in his jacket and put them on. "Well, it goes like this." He shook his head. "Coyote Ugly is . . . when you wake up in the morning with your arm underneath what it was you picked up at the bar the night before, and she . . . or he is so ugly you chew off your arm in order to get away."

Ava cocked her head. "Yeah . . . ," she said, trying to counter the in-joke between the two brothers, "I've been there before."

"Well," he said, as he pulled down his glasses, "then you can understand what it really means."

"No . . . wait," Ava replied. She stepped closer to her husband. "What does it really mean?"

Coyote rolled his hand over his hair and turned sideways. "It means that we might be on a roll, but watch out."

"Watch out for what?"

"Watch out for Coyote Ugly." He pushed them back up. "That's all there is."

"Sounds like boy talk to me."

Coyote laughed. "That's what I said a long time ago."

Another balloon went up that read, "Coyote Fats."

"Now what does that mean?"

"That was my father's name."

"I thought it was Don Coyote."

"Naw . . . that was only his fancy name." He pointed to another bubble. "It means that things will be getting real good soon."

The third bubble read, "Coyote Silk."

Coyote laughed and waved when he finally saw his brother sitting casually under a canopied table.

"Damn it, Coyote . . . what does Coyote Silk mean?" Ava asked, as she grabbed Coyote's arm.

"I have no idea," he answered, "no idea t'all."

When Ava and Coyote reached the table Kid had a bottle of wine waiting for them. Dramatically, he swept his arm around the stadium. "Madame and Monsieur . . . you like?"

Ava ignored Kid's presentation. "You look great, Kid." She pulled him against her body. "I've missed you . . . you silly goose."

"Ahhh . . . the warrior muttering obscentities." He kissed her forehead, leaned back to take in the full view of her smiling face and kissed her on the lips. He glanced over at his brother. "Hope you guys can stick around because Molly and I are getting married tomorrow."

Ava looked around the stadium and park. "How beautiful . . . ," she said, as she turned slowly around, "being married in Paris."

Tuesday pulled Kid into his arms and then reached for Ava.

"I hope you invited Mona," he said, as he messed up Kid's hair.

Kid passed around the wine glasses. "Here's to Mona, and then he lifted up his glass just as Molly flew over the stadium upside down. "And Molly . . ." They yelled at Molly, touched glasses and sipped the wine. Kid picked up the wine bottle and looked at the label. "A superb Pouilly-Fumé . . . don't you think?"

"Von of zee bettah Vouvrays . . . I zink," Ava responded, "alzzo a leetle flabbee 'sround zee nose . . ." She kicked Kid in the shins. "Vat a snob you have becomes, Kid Monday. An' zee war has onlee been over for von day."

Again, Molly flew over the stadium. Kid, Ava and Coyote jumped up. She blew them a kiss. Kid, dressed in the clothes he had worn when he first showed up at May's villa, sat on the back of a chair and filled everyone's glasses. "The Whoa Man gave you quite a ride, heh?" He raised his glass. "And right on target."

"Here's to The Whoa Man," Coyote said.

"And the rest," Ava added.

They emptied their glasses and Coyote refilled them. He leaned back in his chair and tapped his computer. "We watched Molly have her first flying lesson." He touched Ava's arm. "I've probably mentioned this a hundred times but up on Mesa Five, Kid and I could always communicate no matter what." He looked over at his brother and winked. "We were hot back then."

Kid opened a second bottle of Vouvray. "That's why you left when you were seventeen," he said sarcastically. He refilled their glasses. "Right?" He looked at his brother. "You look beat." He sipped his wine as he stared at his younger brother. "Your leg seems to be worse."

"Ahhh . . . I'll be okay."

"Bullshit . . . ," Ava countered. She took Kid's hand. "It was healing so well on the Fifth Mesa, but when we found out you guys were playing around in Paris we just had to join you." She looked up as five bi-planes flew over. "Everything on the Fifth Mesa seems so passé." She took a deep breath. "Look," she said, as she stood up and walked around the table. "Just look at all of this." She grabbed a young man who was walking past their table. "Je t'aime," she said, and kissed him on the cheek.

Coyote jumped up and began to wave to the women. "Bonjour Madame, bonjour Mademoiselle, howdy there Mesdames," he spoke, as he tipped his hat and smiled. "Bonjour . . ."

Ava grabbed her husband and kissed him on the nose. "Je t'aime mon bella Coyote, Je t'aime."

Coyote sat back down and rubbed his leg. A sudden rain squall came up and was gone within minutes. They laughed, cooed, smacked, and sighed and mentally pinched themselves when they couldn't believe where they were or what they were doing. It was all too perfect, and, as they reviewed their situation, they couldn't understand why they hadn't left earlier.

"We were just so fucking serious," Ava said.

"'Life's too mysterious to take it serious,'" Kid quoted.

"Who said that?"

"Beats me . . ."

"I think it was April Fools," Ava said.

Kid stood up, stretched, and sat down. "I know," he said as he fiddled with his wine glass, "how about say, when the air show is over, the four of us rent a motor car and tour France." He shrugged and raised his eyebrows. "Or maybe all of Europe."

Coyote and Ava blinked and looked graciously puzzled.

"Come on," Kid continued, "where do you have to be?"

Ava smiled, as she glanced over at a young couple pushing a double stroller. "Wandering Foot has been completely destroyed," she said, as she sipped her wine.

"I know," Kid answered. "So, there's no place to go except wander around in the past until our present becomes inhabitable again. Or, return to the Fifth Mesa."

"Don't you think we should try and make it livable?" Ava looked into their eyes. "We can't just keep floating around."

"Why not," Kid replied. He patted his trombone. "We want kids and maybe you guys would like some . . . right? I don't think any of us are ready for permanent life on the Fifth Mesa."

Coyote leaned forward, "I'm for the tour." He patted his leg. "It would give my leg a chance leg to heal, and then, perhaps we could travel all over the Third Mesa and eventually find a place somewhere where we could put on an international peace festival."

"I know," Ava said, as she pulled Coyote and Kid in closer to her, "what if we were able to bring all of the people together, from say the beginning, who have tried in some way or another for world peace. Think of it, you guys." She looked into the sky and lifted up her hands. "One big mother fucker of a festival and can you imagine the power? Just the auras alone from all of those heavy hitters would be like putting an entire shield over the Third Mesa." She stepped back and clenched her fists. "Never again . . . would the Third Mesa have to have what it's gone through." She shook her head and smiled. "Never . . ."

Coyote and Kid knew that Ava was onto something. Their attention was distracted by a Bristol two-seater that had dropped out of a hammerhead stall into a twisting dive. When the aircraft finally pulled up, Kid looked over at Ava and Coyote and gave them the thumbs-up. "With the perfect mixture in the ol' Cheyenne Rose, our Fifth Mesa consciousness, and the Himalayan foothills say . . . we'll have peace knocked forever."

"Yeah . . . !" Coyote shouted.

"I think we should have some champagne," Ava announced. "And when Molly comes down we'll sneak off for southern France."

Kid ran into the wine tent and talked the merchant out of his last bottle of 1893 Perrier-Jouet. He returned to the round canopied table with the bottle jammed into an ice bucket. The merchant's son came over, opened the bottle, and filled three champagne saucers with the rare vintage.

"Here's to The Whoa Man's multi-talented orgasmic troupe," Ava proposed. "To Molly, The Flying Tibetan-Apache Ace, the peace festival and our Tour de France."

"Yiiiiiiipppppppeeeee," Coyote shouted, as he jumped into the air and punched the sky. "We're long gone from war." He winced and sat back down.

"Look at that woman fly," Ava said, feeling slightly jealous. "Next time, Kid . . . I want to go up."

After they had finished the bottle, Ava and Coyote agreed to find out about renting an automobile while Kid waited for Molly. Kid walked over to the wine tent and thanked the merchant for the wine and champagne.

The Frenchman looked puzzled as he returned some change to a woman who had just purchased two liters of Vin Ordinaire Blanc. "But . . . ah monsieur, you haven't paid me."

Kid's face turned red. He blinked, shook his head and looked over at Ava and Coyote for help. Coyote turned away and started to whistle. Kid returned his attention to the merchant. "Ahhh . . . listen," he said, as he patted his trombone case. "You see, monsieur, I . . . ah . . . ," he rubbed his chin and closed one eye. "Well . . . I kinda made this all up."

The Frenchman laughed and clapped his hands. "Oh . . . I see,' he replied, as he turned up his hands. "You, of course, must be God . . . I should have known. How stupid of me. And your two companions are Your Son and the Holy Ghost. Or possibly Adam and Eve." He shrugged and looked around for his son. "God never has to pay." He slapped the wooden counter. "Right?" He sighed and closed his eyes. "Please," he continued, "I've had a very busy day, and I realize that you and your friends might have . . . ah . . . possibly drunk a little too much wine. No? so please . . . don't cause any trouble." He nervously looked at his Patek Phillip pocket watch and snapped the case shut. His large liquid brown eyes were almost sympathetic.

Coyote slapped his forehead and motioned for Ava to come over and help. He turned back to Kid and spoke from the side of his mouth. "Get rid of this turkey."

Kid looked as if he had just swallowed his trombone. He gulped and turned aside. "I can't. There's no reverse. You should know that."

"What?" Coyote mumbled. "A wizard without an emergency escape routine." He shook his head. "You're slipping, Kid."

Kid kicked Coyote in the shins. "Cool it," he whispered. "Since we got here I haven't been able to find any supplies for Cheyenne Rose."

The Frenchman leaned across the counter and grabbed Kid's jacket. "Are you Americans?"

Coyote started to tell him about the Third and Fifth Mesas when Ava stepped up to the counter. "Well," he started to explain, "we're from . . . ah . . ."

"You can pay me in dollars," the shopkeeper suggested.

"Dollars?" Coyote yipped, as he started to laugh.

The merchant was slowly becoming perturbed. "Swiss, German, English, Italian . . . ? Just give me anything if you don't have French money."

Ava leaned over the counter, smiled at the wine merchant, and slowly caressed his hand. "Well, you see, monsieur, it's . . . ah . . . this way," she began, as she tried to keep up her smile. "We seem to be from another time period, and . . . well . . . because of the wars . . . ah . . . we no longer have a monetary system . . ."

The merchant rolled his eyes, pulled away, and looked at all three of them. "How did you arrive if you have no money?" he asked.

Ava looked over at Kid for assistance. "Help . . ." she pleaded.

"Damn it Kid," Coyote said, under his breath, "get us out of this mess."

Kid noticed a crowd gathering outside the tent. Someone yelled that the two men dressed in strange clothing were either gypsies or from the circus, and those types were always trying to pull a fast one. "Call the gendarmes," came a voice from the back.

The merchant was beginning to realize that he wasn't going to be paid. He picked up a hammer and started waving it in the air. "I will not allow you to leave my tent without paying me."

"Flash them your credit card," Coyote joked, as he turned to face the crowd.

Kid grabbed his trombone, jumped up on the counter and quickly attempted to take it out of the case. "I'm going to send these people back to the Fifth Century and let them deal with Attila the Hun." He reached for his beaded bottle just as the merchant hit him on the foot with the hammer. Kid yelled, and jumped off the counter. "You rotten little beagle-nosed frog . . ." A woman tried to grab the trombone out of his hands. "Watch yourself, sweet-heart. . . ."

Coyote discovered that Ava had a man locked in a half-nelson. "What are you doing?"

"He pinched my ass."

"And you're going to break his arm?"

"Not unless he apologizes in one of the languages I can under-stand," she answered.

Kid crawled out of the tent on his hands and knees. As soon as he found Ava and Coyote, two policemen came charging into the tent.

"Get us out of here," Coyote demanded.

"I need some room," Kid yelled, as he quickly checked around the grounds. "I need someplace to hide."

"Hey!" Ava shouted, "Look up there . . . Molly's in trouble."

Kid saw that the Sopwith's engine was in flames. "Oh my God," he yelled. He grabbed Coyote's arm. "Make some kind of diversion," he demanded.

Molly was desperately trying to pull the aircraft out from a dive but she wasn't having any luck. Coyote shook his fist at Kid. "Mon-day," he said, as they ducked behind a circus tent near the Etang de Suresnes, "you should be shipped back to the minor leagues."

Kid kept telling himself to remain calm and not to panic. Two women with baby carriages were informing the police where the troublemakers were hiding. Ava grabbed Coyote and started kissing him. "Go on," she yelled to Kid, "get us out of this mess."

Kid grabbed the bottle of elixir and started running up the Route des Tribunes. Whistles were blowing and one of the many boys in the street tried to trip Kid with an extra long bagette. He quickly glanced back to see how his brother and Ava were doing, but the crowd had already sealed them from view. "Good luck," he mumbled, as he leaped over a black dog that was pulling a small bread cart. He tried to find Molly's airplane but he was underneath an awning. The cops were struggling to break through the crowd to get at Ava and Coyote, but the bystanders wouldn't let them through. "Ahhhh . . . leave them alone," a tall man in a long drooping mustache yelled. "Fuck off . . ."

"Yeah, can't you see they're in love?"

The crowd's attitude change was instantaneous. Besides, the real culprit had already taken off leaving this beautiful couple in the lurch. Someone pulled out a wad of Francs, "I'll pay their bill."

"They must be from India . . ."

A paddy wagon pulled up with its staccato siren blurting out its arrival. Coyote glanced up to see ten gendarmes jump out of the wagon and head their way. "Kid," he mumbled under his breath, "it's going to be wonderful celebrating the first days of peace in a Parisian jail."

Kid ran onto the Longchamp track. Three bands were parading around the perimeter, and several airplanes were landing inside the racecourse to refuel. Molly was trying to make it to an open field outside Paris. He jumped onto a Red Cross ambulance, primed his trombone, got down on one knee, and tried to figure out what he should do with the mess he had created. He wasn't certain whether he could find the beginning or the end, but he didn't have enough time for that. He would just have to make something happen, fuck-ups and all. Otherwise, if they got his trombone, all three of them would be stuck in a Parisian jail with Molly down somewhere in the countryside.

"Come on baby," Kid pleaded to his instrument, "I need you more than ever before. Just get us out of here and back into some kind of manageable scenario." He put the trombone to his lips and desperately tried to think where they could have their peace festival. Nothing came to mind. He couldn't think. "All I can do," he said to himself, "is pray for some supreme intervention." He even tried a quick prayer to his mother. Everyone in the stands was pointing either at him or Molly's Sopwith. What he needed more than anything else was an erasure to the Ninth Power, expressivo prestissimo.

Kid blew out the bubble and his Latter Day Peace Oracle came out looking like a skid row watermelon. It was wearing a cheap pair of red-framed sunglasses, striped tights with baggy socks, a cap on backwards that read, Coyote Silk, a mangy looking fur coat, a baseball glove in one hand and an electric guitar in the other. It spoke a strange patois of Western twang and Parisian French; acted as if it had a monstrous hangover, or had decided to slum around a little with the peasants. It thumbed its nose at the crowd, mooned them in four exaggerated directions, and then grabbed Kid by the scruff of the neck and pulled him into the air to avoid being captured by the gendarmes who had reached the ambulance.

At thirty feet it began to change, and at fifty its metamorphosis had filled the entire oval. Four shafts of light stretched out in the Hopi sunrise as the center began to expand in a mixture of colors. Within the center a mandala of human faces began to emerge— flashing out everyone who had ever thought, dreamed, and acted in the consciousness of peace. And then, slowly, it began to take on the shape of an atomic explosion—the mushroom cloud building out of its womb—engulfing the entire sky. There were cries and gasps, but no one could leave—being consumed by what they thought to be the end of the earth. The light kept expanding as the stadium was filled with a pale green mist, and then, as if the air show had never happened, everything that Kid had created back on the river was frozen like a still photograph, and then gone. Somewhere, out there in the seedling handsome of his imagination, a new medicine show was beginning to take shape, but he had no idea what it was or how it would turn out. Once again, the destiny of peace was up for grabs.

Kid Monday's medicine show was a ragged blending of Ouzi-hoopla that included, in layers, a former world skydiving championship (circa undetermined), bits and pieces of the 1920's Paris Air Show, a Native American Powwow, a white water rodeo, and, of course, a peace festival. All of which were taking place at the same time at Wandering Foot.

17

Coyote and Ava tagged Kid's peace fandango The Double B-Czar-B Peace Festival because it started out so strangely punch-drunk. Nevertheless, they jumped right into the festivities by signing up for the skydiving contest. By some miracle, Kid had also managed to clear out the wreckage from the war, but he had missed a few blown-up tanks and trucks which were reminders of what could still happen.

Besides the skydivers, the pilots from the Paris Air Show, the white water rodeoists, Wandering Foot was filled with the strangest collection of peace lovers, bar none. He had not missed anyone who had in some way dedicated his or her life to the cause. He had the martyrs, the ridiculed, the stoned, those who had been burned-at-the-stake, the crucified, the gassed, and the slaughtered. There were the bearded and the robed, the bald and the fat, the emaciated, the wild-eyed and long-haired. There were also the few who had been praised and honored by the more peace loving cultures; and then, snuggled in between all of those celebrities were those who made up the basic cellular divinity of life: farmers, poets, road runners, sweet ass'd angels, mystical pole vaulters, banjo pickers, exiles, slaves, dreamers, drifters and folk singers. All of them having at one time prayed far beyond their own palaces and dungeons for world peace. The stands were also filled with the more traditional religionists: Moslems, Jews, fire worshipping Zorastrians, Shintoists, Sikhs, Jains, Christians, Native American Shamans, African animists and Buddhists. It was as if a giant computer had spun through the course of human history to extract those who had been crazy enough to stand up for that one dream. Even the repentant and born again were included.

Prayer ceremonies were being conducted, a peace pipe was lit and slowly passed around the stadium, a jazz band was parading around the grounds along with story tellers and folk musicians. When the sky divers realized that a peace festival was going on, they decided that each dive would, in some way, reflect a passage of world peace, and that the winner's purse would be offered for future festivals. Everyone seemed to be in an extraordinary state of higher consciousness, except for Ava and Coyote who were pacing back and forth in their dressing room.

"How much time?" Ava asked Coyote, as she looked out the window at the hot air balloons that were being readied to take some of the spectators up to watch the sky diving performances.

Coyote checked his wrist computer. "We've got about an hour or so before we're scheduled to dive."

"I'm scared," Ava answered, as she once again started pacing the small cubicle. "I don't know what made us sign up for the sky-diving competition, and everyone imaginable is out there except Kid and Molly." She stopped and gazed blankly at her husband. "I can't imagine what happened to them."

Coyote reached over and put his arm around his wife. "Come on, Ava, I've never known Kid to miss a parade, especially his own."

Ava looked into Coyote's dark brown eyes. "I don't understand it," she answered, as she shook her head, "he was able to slip us out of that paddy wagon, pull off this show, and now they've vanished." She turned away. "Maybe Molly crashed before Kid could get her out of that plane."

Coyote tried to locate them on his computer, but there was too much interference from all the high-powered minds inside the stadium. He pulled on his jumpsuit, looked at himself in the mirror and winked. "Coyote," he said, "don't you ever die."

Ava opened the tent flap and walked outside. "Look at this, Coyote," she said, turning back, "it's so much better than I could have imagined." She closed her eyes as she tried to pull everyone's spirit into her body.

Coyote looked around. The sun was setting and the hills were washed in a patina of soft apricot and purple. He stepped back into the tent and picked up their gear. He heard the roar of the crowd as two enormous flocks of doves were released. "At least Kid had the smarts to clean up Wandering Foot." He looked around the canyon. "It's almost like it was before."

"You mean when it was your father's reservation?"

"Yes," Coyote replied.

Ava kissed Coyote. "Here's to world peace, Tues."

Coyote pulled Ava against his slender body and returned the kiss. "I love you, Ava, and for our number, I think we should . . . or . . . if possible . . . ah . . . we should try to consummate our reunion plus maybe even make a kid or two." He looked into her eyes and smiled. "Whatcha think?"

"Get out of here," Ava answered, as she tried to see how serious he was. "Come on . . . we couldn't do that."

Coyote's eyes were suddenly filled with the sunset. He laughed. "We could try . . ."

She backed away. "Coyote, it wouldn't be proper."

"Whoa," Coyote answered. "This is a peace festival, isn't it?"

"Yes, but not that kind, my dear." She gave Coyote a playful shove. "Do you think you . . . ah . . . could . . ." She punched his arm. "Ah . . . get out of here, Tues."

*　　*　　*　　*　　*

As Ava and Coyote were preparing for their aerial performance, Kid and Molly were sitting in the middle of the desert with their heads buried in despair. The Sopwith Camel that he had created for her flying debut was smashed nose-up thirty miles east of Wandering Foot. Molly, wearing high, lace-up leather boots, fan-tailed riding

147

britches, a fur-lined flight jacket, and a silk scarf draped across her shoulders, was looking into Kid's face—trying to stare some good sense into him. "Kid Monday," she said, as she wiped away a tear, "why are you being so stubborn and unimaginative?" She leaned in closer—hoping to find the answer somewhere inside the lagoons of his green eyes. "You saved my tail and created the peace festival, so why this?"

Kid lifted the scarf from Molly's shoulders and wrapped it around his neck. "Molly, I told you before that I had to use every drop of my magic formula to create the festival, get your ass out of that junk heap over there and keep Ava and Coyote from being hauled off to the Paris hoosegow." He gave her a halfhearted smile. "I'm not really sure what happened at the Air Show. I remember . . . I really tried for something special. I had this image of Ava and Coyote skydiving through my head, and there was the air show, and some Native Americans and I'm not even sure where the festival is." He looked sheepishly at Molly. "I tried for the Ninth Mesa, but I kept seeing Wandering Foot superimposed without any of the destruction." He shrugged. "Maybe I did or maybe not. But, I did try for some kind of healing for Coyote's ancestral home."

Molly took his hand. "I appreciate what you've done, Kid, and I'm sure the festival is going to be a great success. But, I'd like to be there, y'know?"

Kid walked over to the two seater and looked at the motor that was hanging off the fuselage like a fly-specked tongue out of a bush-whacked buffalo. "Damn it Molly, don't you think that I would like to be there?" He kicked at the broken wheel.

Molly jumped up and ran over to the cockpit of the bi-plane. "Well hotshot, I'm not going to give up." She grabbed Kid's trombone. "Where's the mojo juice?"

Kid's mind leaped out faster than his tired body. All he could do was fall back against the fuselage as Molly ran out through the sage brush. "Hey," he yelled, "put it back!"

"Where's the beaded bottle?" she yelled.

"I used it all up."

"Baloney."

"It's true," he answered.

"Where's the spare?" she demanded.

"Spare?" he replied, almost laughing. "Wizards of my caliber don't need spares."

148

"Ha!" Molly exclaimed, "it sounds like you've got your honorable wizardry lost up you own cosmic butthole." She turned her back on him. "I don't need spares," she mimicked, in a high, shrill voice. She put the trombone together.

"Molly Rose," he yelled, "don't mess with it."

"And shit and two make eight," she answered back. "That's just male crapola and you know it."

Kid tried to catch her by feinting to one side, and then dashing at her from the other. She was much too quick for him and kept her distance. "Come on," he begged, "even if you could make it work, all you could possibly wing out would be a toy Sopwith Pup that looked like it had seen twenty-two miles of detoured orphans."

Molly thumbed her nose at Kid. "You old dime store Republican," she yelled. "I'm going to make you eat those words, bullshit and all." She opened up the case and found the beaded bottle in one of the velvet lined pockets. "Okay hotshot . . . let's see what this famous trickster-elixir can do." She wagged her ass as she poured out one small drop into the palm of her hand. "It don't look like any sacred hot sauce to me, Kid." She tasted the liquid. "Come on rodeo boy, this tastes just like it came from a gallon jug of Ragmart's generic shampoo."

"The hell you say," he answered as he walked around in a semicircle, sliding the scarf back and forth. "It's my own secret formula, and coveted by every wizard within five mesas."

Molly offered him a generous raspberry, dolentemente.

"Hey, I promise."

"Well, your honorable wizardry," she said, as she slowly bowed to him, "I bet I could come up with something much better than this."

"Ha," he exclaimed, as he turned his back and walked away. He stood by the biplane, lost in how beautiful she had looked when Molly was zipping around in the Paris sky. He slammed his fist into the palm of his hand. "Damn," he said, under his breath. "I just needed more time." Suddenly he spun around when he realized that Molly was serious about making up her own formula. "Wait, don't even try," he shouted. He raced back. "It would be like using diesel fuel for mouth wash."

Molly calmly reached into her shoulder bag and extracted a small bottle of shampoo. "Honestly, Mister Monday, I really thought you had more class."

"Come on, Molly, give it up," he replied, as he began to strut in front of her. "It took me years of training on the Fifth Mesa before I could even create anything close to a miracle. And then, I had all of my old man's expertise, Mesa Five consciousness, plus the magic trombone."

'Blah, blah, blah," she answered.

"Well, go ahead, and see how difficult it is to be a wizard."

"Yeah . . . I've heard that line before." She turned the trombone upside down.

Kid sat down next to the Sopwith and leaned back against the tire. "You'd better hurry up because it'll be dark soon."

"Just watch me." Molly emptied the shampoo into Kid's bottle. "Now, that should give it a good smooth base." She looked into her bag and found a bottle of mouth wash. "Hey, a clean breath for my maiden voyage." She dumped it in with shampoo. "What else have I got?" She emptied her bag on the ground. "Alka Seltzer . . . in they go. A small vial of ginseng and royal jelly. Dump it in, sister. Artificial tears . . . why not. My last bottle of nail polish . . . it should do something in there." She looked at Kid. "Well, I guess that's it. Any suggestions, commodore?"

Kid grimaced when she stuck the trombone into the sandy dirt. He started to move.

"Keep your distance, pard, or I'll bury this one-legged tuba so deep into the ground that it will take five geological upheavals and six teams of drunken archaeologists just to retrieve one simple melody."

Kid looked into the sky. He half expected to see buzzards flying overhead—circling the prey for the big takeover. Instead, he heard a meadowlark whip out an eleven syllable song which, at that moment, seemed like the only good omen of the evening. He reached into his coat pocket and took out a small silver vial. "Here, use some of this," he said, as he casually tossed her the container.

"What!" Molly snatched it out of the air. "Holding out on me?" She wagged her finger as she studied the design engraved on the side. "And we were just about to get married." She unscrewed the cap. "What is it?"

Kid knelt down, slapped his old cap onto his head as the evening wind started to pick up. "It's a prayer bottle from the old Cowboy Buddha Hotel, back when our dads' were hanging out . . . together. They kept one in the meditation room, and every so often it would be filled with oil, blessed, and given to the one person who they felt lived within the spirit of oneness." He shrugged, and stuffed his hands into the pockets of his blue tweed jacket. "My old man gave it to me just before he split."

The sunset had wrapped itself around Molly with a blue-peach light centered on the vial. "Hey, I remember hearing something like that." She looked up at Kid with a smile that seemed to transform her frustration. "I've heard so many stories about those guys." She stepped closer to Kid and squatted with her knees apart. She rubbed the container, put it against her cheek and eventually kissed it. "When I was a little girl my dad used to tell me stories about the Cowboy Buddha Hotel." She rubbed her nose and looked up to see a swallow flash over Kid's head. "What a bunch of hotshot rene-gades." She fell back on her butt. "Wow!" A smile had torqued an opening between them that wouldn't leave. "I love you, Kid."

Kid stayed back as he took in the scenery. At that moment it didn't seem to matter what was about to happen because all he wanted to do was hold Molly, leave everything else behind, and fly off somewhere. He fiddled with his cap and then jammed it on back-wards. "Careful . . . when you open it," he said softly, "it's very powerful."

"Yeah, yeah," she replied, as she watched his face. At that moment he seemed extremely young, yet very ancient at the same time. She felt like giving up, but something kept pushing her on. "I can tell that it's very old, Kid." She winked, and walked back to the trombone.

"It should only take one drop to do the job."

She emptied the bottle, shrugged, and looked back at him. "Jus' in case . . ."

Kid slapped his forehead. "Molly, Molly, Molly." He walked around in a tight circle as he tried not to think about what could possibly happen. "Good luck, kiddo."

Molly slipped the trombone out of the ground and wiped it clean with a pocket hanky.

"You okay?" he asked.

"Yeah, I'm fine."

He walked back to the Sopwith. "I'll be right over here if you need me."

"Thanks, but I won't."

Kid dumped some sand out of his coat pocket. "We could spend

151

the night here, I suppose," he said, not quite loud enough for Molly to hear. "I'm sure there's a few drops of fuel left to get a fire started." He found an old dried apricot stuck in the bottom of the lining. "I could make a fruit salad."

Molly looked a little knock-kneed. She tested the space around her as she said a prayer to herself and whoever might be listening: The Great Spirit, God, The Great Mother, The Holy People, all of the Holy Highs from Gandhi Dancer, her father and step-dad, Jonquil Rose, jus' one more cowboy, and even Kid. No, especially Kid. When she was ready for her debut, she put the image, exactly the way she wished it to be, into her mind, and then blew, with her eyes closed in the sweetness of making love, out her first bubble. There wasn't even a respectful silence from the frogs and crickets. There wasn't even the tiniest flash of lightning from the Fourth Mesa. Kid cringed and Molly sighed. She opened up her eyes to see the soggiest of bubbles in the history of wizardry flop out, sail only a few feet and then crash into the Sopwith's torn-off wing. Kid buried his head into his arms.

"Fuck," she moaned, as she dug her boots into the sand. She didn't want to look disappointed and she could feel that Kid was desperately trying to keep from intervening. She jammed the slide into the sand. "Go ahead and laugh, see if I care."

"Hey, I'm not."

"Bullshit." Molly walked off. When she came to a scrub juniper she turned back. "I'm not going to be intimidated, you'll see." She walked back. "Any suggestions," she asked, which sounded more like a demand.

Kid cleared his throat and picked at a piece of fabric from the broken wing. "Well," he began, as he glanced at her, "don't be so timid. Give it all you've got with determinato." He raised his arms and faced her. "You're holding a trombone up there in front of everyone, see . . . so act like you really care, and don't be afraid to show some arrogance." He moved closer. "None of this cutesy little girl delicatimente shit."

Molly cringed, but stood her ground. "Okay . . . okay . . ."

He thumped his chest. "And listen to what's going on in here. When you put that instrument up for all of the Holy People, the Holy Highs and even those on the Fourth Mesa to see, your heart has got to be pure with just that one pure image of what you want to create. Right? Nothing else. You can't be competing or envious,

Molly. You've got to kick everything out but your heart and your dreams and then go right down . . . way down after it . . . wherever it might be and drag it up." He bent down and grabbed a handful of dirt. "And don't be afraid to get dirty and mean. And then, that thing in there, whatever it is, has got to come out because you're calling it to you. It's your creation and you're giving it life. And then, BOOM, send it out into the world with robusto." He shook his fists and did a few quick jumps. "You're a natural, Molly Rose, so challenge your ideas and make a believer out of them."

Molly was nodding her head as she ran the slide back and forth. "Okay . . . okay . . ."

"And one more thing," he added, as he turned his back on her and then quickly spun around. "Remember the landscaping of balances, and don't be afraid to laugh and growl at the same time." He jumped into the cockpit and waved his arms like he was conducting an orchestra. "Let's get to work."

"Okay," Molly replied emphatically. "I'll just do that." She walked back to the place where she felt the most comfortable. She touched the trombone and closed her eyes as she tried to think about what she really wanted to create. Her face was tilted to the fading light and she remained in that position for what seemed like a long time. Finally, she opened her eyes, blinked and faced Kid. "I've got it."

"Good!" he shouted. "Hang onto it."

"I'm not sure it's a duplicate, but it'll get us out of here."

"Hey, don't worry about it." He looked all around the sky. "Just get us up there." He laughed, and raised his arms. "To the peace festival and away from this ad infinitum country." He hummed a tune as if it were the music for a commercial.

Molly stayed carefully inside her thoughts. She had the image and all she needed was the energy and spirit. A soft breeze was blowing. She looked up and saw Kid wrap her scarf around his neck. That made her feel better.

"Be happy," he yelled, "don't frown."

Molly swallowed and then executed a fast dance to loosen up. She could feel it building inside, and she knew that she had a hold of something really big. Maybe, even monumental. Two deep knee bends, and then she slowly turned to face the sunset and the evening star. She twirled the trombone, set her tongue just the way her grandmother would do when training a horse, and then she called out, one by one, the names of the missing Holy Highs. She took a deep breath, and for the second time blew out her vision.

"Geronimo!" Kid whispered, not wanting to disturb Molly. "You've got it, you've got it,' he coaxed, as he leaned over the side of the fuselage. "I can see it coming."

The bubble was flat and waxy and looked as if it had been pressed out through a giant wringer. For a second, Kid thought that something had suddenly gone wrong, but, upon closer examination, he could tell by its size and color that it was in good health. As soon as it cleared the bell, its full colors started to develop and within seconds it looked like an intricately woven Persian rug. He glanced at Molly, but she acted as if it were exactly what she wanted. "A carpet?" he asked himself. Molly clenched her fists as she watched it sail over her head. It did three flips and obediently pulled up in front of her. She stepped back, dusted off her hands, looked over at Kid and flipped out a thumb. "Don't be intimidated, Kid," she said, as she lovingly examined her creation, "come on over."

"Whoa," Kid exclaimed, as he jumped down and slowly approached Molly's creation. He wasn't exactly sure what it was, and he was secretly worried that she would be bummed out if it didn't work. It looked two-dimensional, but when he walked over, the colors started to vibrate as if it were alive and there was a bright green light around the edge. It was rectangularly shaped with a circular center. "Hey . . . ," Kid exclaimed, when he finally saw what it was. "It's your sandpainting." He leaned over to examine the central figure. "Yeah . . . there's Buddha Shooting Way, and there's Pollen Boy, Holy Man and Holy Woman, Jesus, Lao-tsu, and Martin Luther King and his dream speech." He knelt down and traced his fingers over King's words.

Molly carefully wiped down the trombone with a soft chamois and put it back into its case. "It's my own peace festival," she said, as she slipped her arm over his shoulder. "The Gandhi Dancer . . ."

"It's beautiful, but . . . well . . . what can it . . . she . . . do?" He leaned back and tried to avoid her eyes. "I mean . . ."

"Ah yes," she interrupted, "you would like to know how it's going to get us out of this mess . . . right?"

"Yeah," he replied, "that's what I had in mind." A huge lump of fear jumped into his throat. He stepped away from her. "I mean . . ." He glanced back at the Sopwith.

"You said that once before." Molly stood admiring her work.

"I can tell that you don't think this baby will fly."

Kid took several breaths as he tried to remain calm. "Breathe deeply," he told himself, "just remember that you are a Holy Person and you're here on a mission." He squatted down next to Molly's Gandhi Dancer and realized that all of the people inside were three dimensional. He also thought Buddha Shooting Way motioned for him to step inside. He looked back at Molly. "What's going on?"

"Go on . . ."

Kid stood up and noticed that the sandpainting had become a cube, and, as soon as he stepped inside, it lost its edges until he was standing inside a sphere. "Whoa," Kid exclaimed, as he quickly glanced around. "This thing's a spook show."

"Look who's talking," Molly answered, as she stepped in next to Kid. She said something to Pollen Boy and then turned back to Kid.

"Yikes," Kid replied, "these Holy People are alive!"

"You still don't get it?"

Kid stared at the Holy People. "You're from the Hall of Fame . . . right?"

They nodded. Pollen Boy stepped toward Kid. "We're on a temporary leave of absence," he laughed, shyly.

"How are we going to get out of here?"

"If you'll observe, Kid Monday," Buddha Shooting Way said, "we're already floating toward the festival."

Kid looked down. "Yo!" he shouted, as he stepped back. Below them was the Sopwith Camel. He turned to Molly. "This is some enlightened wallop you whipped up on your first try." He looked back at Molly's guests. "Hi . . . I'm Kid . . . Mona's son."

They laughed.

He shrugged and looked around the capsule. "Great little ship you've got here, Molly." He looked over at the escaped Holy People. "What can she do?"

"Anything Molly wants," Lao-tsu answered.

Kid rolled his eyes and gulped. "Well, I guess it's just one of those amazing nights where anything goes." Molly was speaking with Confucius. He couldn't tell how fast they were flying. All he wanted was for them to be at the festival before it was over, and hopefully, if she still wanted, get married. He saw a flash of light on the horizon. "Look Molly," Kid said, "that must be it."

Martin Luther King suddenly emerged. He reached over and

155

shook Kid's hand. "Brother Monday."

"Brother King," Kid answered.

"Molly," the Reverend added, as he reached across the capsule.

"Doctor King, I'm so happy that you could be here," Molly replied.

Doctor King sat down and looked at Kid. "Earlier, Buddha Shooting Way and I were talking things over, and we decided that it would be ah . . . better . . . for your brother, Tuesday, if you didn't show up."

Kid rocked back in his chair. "What!"

Holy Woman sat down next to him. "It's not like it sounds," she said, as she touched his hand. He jerked it away.

"It's not?" He looked over at Molly. "What's going on?"

Molly shrugged and looked at Buddha Shooting Way. "I don't know."

Buddha Shooting Way moved closer to Kid. "Except for a few congential anomalies, the festival is perfect and it's going to accomplish a great deal toward world peace." He glanced over at Doctor King. "However, we all thought that it would help your brother if you stayed away."

The other Holy People nodded. "That's right," they said in unison.

Kid was hurt and he didn't know how to react. He sighed and looked up at Doctor King. "But I . . ."

"We realize that you wouldn't do anything to hurt your brother," Doctor King said, "and we know how much love you have for him. But, he needs to build up his confidence, and if you showed up with this," he looked around the Gandhi Dancer, "it would just blow him away." He touched Kid's shoulder. "Don't you see?"

"But what if . . . ," Kid started to say.

"It won't," Holy Man answered.

"Trust us," Pollen Boy added.

Kid was looking from one Holy High to the next. "Wow," he said, as he leaned back. "I know the festival isn't perfect, but I had such little time to put it together."

"It is perfect," Holy Woman replied, "and we're confident that it will be a great success."

"But . . . it would be nice to . . . ah . . . see it," Kid answered.

"We can watch it from Mesa Five," Molly said, as she took Kid's hand. "They're absolutely right about Coyote."

Kid jumped up. "But how will he know that we haven't deserted him?"

Doctor King sat down and stretched out his legs. "He will just have to believe . . ."

"In himself," Lao-tsu added.

"They'll rise to the occasion," Doctor King added.

"It will be a glorious festival," Holy Man confirmed.

Kid sat down and rubbed his eyes. "Wow . . . I suppose you're right." He looked up. "For the past ten years all I've thought about was being with him . . ."

"But," Buddha Shooting Way said, "you didn't." He walked around in a circle. "Just let him be."

Kid closed his eyes and tried to figure out what the Holy Man meant. He didn't join Coyote because he didn't want to fight in the war. He looked over at Molly and suddenly realized that she and Ava had remained on the Third Mesa. That they had chosen to stay no matter what happened. At least until it came right down to the wire. He stood up and walked around the capsule. He felt confused, but he knew, deep within himself, that they were right. That Coyote had to pull off the festival, no matter what. He sat back down. "You're right." He smiled, and looked at each Hall of Famer. "But then, how could I argue with you guys." He laughed and looked over at Molly. "Is this okay with you?"

"Of course." She took his hand. "Ava and Coyote will be just fine."

Kid bit his lower lip and looked across the capsule at Doctor King. "You know, I would do anything for Tues."

"Then do this for him."

"Besides, we've got to get back to The Hall," Four Winds said.

The Holy Highs laughed. "That's right," Jesus added, "we've been following you guys around since you hightailed it out of Wandering Foot."

"Really?" Molly asked, as she put her arms around Holy Man and Holy Woman. "I had this strange feeling that we were being followed."

Confucius looked at his rose gold Bulova wrist watch. "We've been AWOL now for almost . . ."

"Who cares," Pollen Boy interrupted, "we're heading back home." He touched Kid's shoulder. "If . . . you give us the okay."

"Let's go," Kid answered. He nodded his head. "But maybe we

could just hang out . . . say . . . on the outskirts just to make sure."

"No sweat," Jesus replied. He looked over at Buddha Shooting Way. "Right?"

"Sure thing."

Holy Woman clapped her hands. "All right . . . mission completed." She hugged Molly and kissed her cheek. "You're gonna love the Fifth Mesa . . . honey."

"I'm anxious to see how Mom . . . ah . . . Mona is doing," Kid said, as he put his arm around Molly.

"Oh, I think the children were able to get her back on track," Holy Woman answered. "With a little help from Spider Woman."

"I hope so," Kid replied. He gazed out through the capsule. "Coyote," he said quietly, "I think I've just been shanghaied, but I'm sure you'll knock 'em dead." He laughed at what he had just said. Then, he turned around and looked at Molly and The Holy Highs, "keep the faith, brother . . . keep the faith."

Ava was upset. Some of their old skydiving buddies had gotten together, figured out an aerial scheme, and then proceeded to set up an **18** electronic betting system so that everyone in the stadium could participate. Six acrobatic teams had been formed, betting cards made up and distributed and the money collected was to go for the Third Mesa orphans. Coyote was also worried, but he was more concerned about Molly and Kid. Everyone in the audience seemed to think the betting was a good idea since it was getting late, the speeches and sermons had been going on for a long time, and a little action would be just the thing to liven up the festivities. Some electronic whizzes were able to assemble an aerial seismograph that could read auras transmitted from the skydivers' bodies which seemed to be a foolproof system since the performers would know within themselves just how good they really were.

The aerial seismograph was an intricate contraption that had been made from salvaged military parts: computers, sensors, monitors, radar dishes, gauges and wires.

The volunteer judges went up in hot air balloons to evaluate the skydivers' manuevers, and those who suffered from acrophobia, stayed on the ground to judge the landings. The team that was scheduled to jump before Ava and Coyote had, at one time, been the first couple to perfect the intricate Double Inverse Paraboloid to the Ninth Symphonic Boogaloo—Jeff Yamamoto and Heidi Wingo, former Third Mesa title holders. It was going to be very difficult for any of the other diving teams to outscore them.

The first couple was waiting in the center of the stadium for the double-winged Spad to take them up for their first go-around.

Ava watched the plane land and roll to a stop. "Damn it Coyote, I have this feeling that Kid and Molly have gone back to the Fifth Mesa." She turned back to her husband. "I just can't seem to shake it."

Coyote looked puzzled as he watched the two contestants being strapped into wing seats. "Why would they want to do a dumb thing like that?"

Ava adjusted the elastic cuffs around her boots. "How should I know, but I wish you'd do something about our two lost friends.

Coyote waved to another skydiving team. He wanted to go out into the center of the arena and hang out with the other contestants. He mumbled something about fussy women, and walked back into the tent. "Okay, okay, don't race your motor." He sat down at a folding table and took off his wrist computer. "Maybe this will work now." He banged it on the table. "I tried earlier but Kid's frequency was jammed." He looked back at Ava. "He's definitely acting like a man in love." Coyote started punching in the information they needed to locate Kid and Molly. "What's the date? And when did we last see them? It was Nineteen hundred and Ninety—and Nineteen hundred and Twenty. Okay? He left the Fifth Mesa around Two thousand and something . . . give or take a few for Fifth Mesa Space Case Time." He finished the calculations, took some alligator clips and hooked his computer onto a large screen that was set up in their tent to watch the festival events. He made several adjustments as sudden glitches flashed horizontally across the monitor. "They're either traveling incognito, evaporated into cosmic riddles, or lost in waltz time somewhere in Vienna."

"You don't have the antenna out," Ava said, as she reached over and flipped a switch that shot two small wires out from the back of the computer. She sat down on a portable camp stool. "What

160

frequency are you on?"

A huge roar came from the crowd. The spotlights had been turned on and they were following the Spad as it lined up for the first drop.

Coyote was trying all of the frequencies. Suddenly, there was a brief flash on the screen. "Look at this, Ava, here's something on this frequency that only Navajo medicine men use." He tapped the screen.

Ava fine-tuned the larger screen and adjusted the controls that lead to the outside dish. "How's that?"

"We've got it." He pushed a key that locked in Gandhi Dancer's position. "Look, they're flying over the Fifth Mesa." He zoomed in on the image. "What the hell . . ." Immediately, he started to sweat so he unzipped his jumpsuit and pulled it down around his waist. He glanced at Ava. "We've got them."

The center of the screen was filled with Molly's creation. "It looks like one of the sandpaintings Molly was creating at your old Shoin," Ava said. "Didn't you ever see it?"

"No, but look at all those Holy Highs." He started calling out their names. "Buddha Shooting Way, Doctor King, Lao-tsu . . ."

"I wonder why they didn't stop here," Ava interrupted.

"Maybe the festival wasn't good enough for them," Coyote answered.

It's because of the gambling," Ava exclaimed.

"Bullshit."

"It's the skydivers . . ."

"Get out of here, Ava," Coyote answered, as he leaned back. "Kid wouldn't care about that."

Ava pointed at the screen. "Those people would, and Molly and Kid are embarrassed."

"Hey, hold your horses, woman, Kid's trying to say something."

"Damn it," she shouted, "you should have stopped them."

"Stop who?"

"Your friends from setting up the gambling scheme."

"Oh yeah . . . now they're my friends."

Ava sat down and turned up the volume. "Shhh . . ."

Kid's face filled the screen. "Hey, Ava and Tues, I hope you're picking this up." Kid looked at Molly and Doctor King. "We're up here in . . . ah . . . this flying sandpainting that Molly created from Cheyenne, and we're flying back to the Fifth Mesa. I'm sorry about the mix-up in Paris, you guys, but Molly's Sopwith crashed as I was trying to get her into Wandering Foot for the peace festival. And then, I ran out of elixir so Molly got all pissed off at me and called up this sandpainting to rescue us." Kid smiled, and raised one eyebrow. "It's really weird and I'll have to explain it all later, but it looks like these Holy Highs are hell-bent-for-leather to get back to The Hall of Fame, and since we're just hitchin' a ride it looks like we'll have to miss the festival." He looked back at Molly. "Molly says she's certain that the festival is really great and we're sorry that we can't make it." He leaned back and cupped his ear. "Oh yes . . . one more thing, the wedding is still on, and as soon as you guys can get up here we'll have it." Kid turned back to Doctor King. "Hey Tues and Ava," Kid said when he returned, "Doctor King says he would be more than pleased to perform the ceremony. How does that grab you?" Kid had the camera pan the room. "Can you see all of these people we're riding with. Hot stuff . . . heh?" He waved, and Molly blew them a kiss.

Coyote flipped off the screen "What a couple of assholes."

Ava remained seated. "It's not their fault."

"Bullshit . . ."

"Coyote," Ava said, as she stood up, "It will be . . . okay."

"Fuckum!" He grabbed a beer and walked outside. There was a huge roar as one of the teams took off in a Bristol. Coyote slipped under the stands and headed for the river. When he came to the bank he stopped, kicked at a few rocks and slowly meandered up river. "What a fuckin' hotdog asshole he is." He kicked at an empty mortar casing, and walked with his head down until he was away from the lights. He stopped when he was left with only the river noise, the crickets, and the wind sifting through the cottonwoods. "It's the way it's always been," he thought, as he picked a stem of grass and jammed it into his mouth. "Kid always comes out smelling like a rose, no matter what. And I always took the shit, just like now." He shook his head as he looked at the stars. "Kid will get all of the credit for putting on the peace festival, and I'll take all the crap for having it turn into a gambling casino." He closed his eyes and tried not to think, but he couldn't make his mind stop. There was just too much anger from years back. "Well fuck it, and fuck you Kid, and Mona, and all of your asshole, mother fuckin' Holy People." He slammed his fist into the night. "Fuck all of you and the dog dick you rode in on!" He stumbled on a rock and almost fell. He was tired, and he could feel his weariness like too many dirt roads. "Fuck all of your Holy Highs," he shouted again. He turned toward the stadium, "and all of you dumb fucks praying for peace. What a fuckin' joke. You're probably fleecing each other's pockets right now." He sat down on a large rock and beat on his head. He heard a roar from the stadium and he knew that it was time for him and Ava to get their gear. He couldn't feel anything about the routine they had worked out. It seemed so flat and stupid. If only he could think of something else, something that could absolutely knock their socks off. He listened to his thoughts and then chuckled as he discovered that he was hearing The Whoa Man's ideas about wanting to create another moon. Sure why not? "Perhaps I could beat him to it," he heard himself say out loud. "Maybe Ava and I could do it?" He began to slowly walk downstream. His leg was hurting but it almost felt good. It reminded him of the war and it just felt fucking good. Perhaps, because it didn't make him think that he was just a total failure. That's all he had. The rest was all dog shit. But he did have the memory of saving that kid's life. Maybe he did. Maybe he made it all up except the pain. But he wasn't a failure. The fear of that reality reminded him of dead meat—of looking down into the black hole and feeling nothing except that he was next. And then . . . so what? He felt the smoothness of the air and he wanted to swallow it whole. All of it. The entire night. Suck it all in and keep it there like a whiskey fire and then ride it into Kid's easy laughter. His smile. His beautiful sweet face. What a fucker. How he could laugh at everything was a miracle of miracles. How he could smile and joke and let it all fly by. He came close to feeling what it was that Kid laughed about, but then the smallest of a tear broke loose and ended the thought. He chuckled and wiped it away. Damn! He almost felt it. He shook his head as he saw The Whoa Man and Kid laughing and being laughed at. They didn't care, did they? They didn't even give a fiddler's fuck. Not because they couldn't but because they really did know. And both of them were miraculously blessed to be happy. To blow up the moon or create a Wagnerian circus when a simple haiku would have been more sufficient. Or the peace festival that was more like a home town carnival with just the usual cast of characters. Who cares? Hey Mister Coyote? At least they were having a good time and for one moment there was peace. That was it. Nothing more. He laughed and turned full circle. Molly's Gandhi

Dancer seemed to be hovering way over near the Fifth Mesa and Kid was probably telling jokes to Jesus, Doctor King, Buddha Shooting Way and the rest of the Holy High gang. And they were probably all laughing and maybe gambling besides. Taking bets on what he and Ava were going to do. Ha!

Coyote jumped into the air and punched the night. "Damn it!" he yelled. "The Gandhi Dancer looks just like a moon." He rocked back on his heels and shook his fists. "That's it . . ." He spun around and dropped to his knees. "Now I've finally got it, and Kid . . . stand back and watch my smoke."

*　　*　　*　　*　　*

A tall black man opened the tent flap. "It's just about time," he said, "Heidi and Jeff have just gone up."

"Thanks," Ava answered, as she followed him out the door. "Have you seen my husband?"

"Tuesday Coyote?" he answered.

"Yes . . ."

He shook his head. "Not since he helped us rig up the seismograph."

"That shit," Ava said. "Thanks anyway." She paced back and forth as she tried to think how she could do the routine alone. "No way," she said to herself, "no way."

"Hey!" Coyote shouted, as he came scooting underneath the stands. "Let's go."

Ava watched him in silence. "Are you okay?" She cocked her head and kept her distance.

"Yeah . . . I'm fine." He took her hands and kissed her cheek. "I'm okay." Nodding, he looked into her dark eyes. "Really."

"Number Five team has just gone up," Ava said, as she looked up. "They're going to be really hot."

Coyote kissed her. "Don't worry, we'll be so good we'll drive them into the ultimate question mark. How did they do it?" He hugged her and ran his fingers through her curly short hair.

After they assembled their equipment, they walked over to the judges' platform to see Heidi and Jeff drop out of the Spad at five thousand feet, stabilize, and then slip into a Flying Double Curl with a Folium Glide. They maintained that position until they had the audience on its feet, and then they reached between their legs, grabbed each other's wrists, and immediately flipped into a Helical

G Force 7 Yin and Yang Spin. Five seconds, and then Heidi took Jeff's ankles and spun onto his lap which put them into a Horizontal Whip and Roll Number Nine Brahma Rip. Ten seconds, as they waited for the centrifugal force to push them apart, and when they were in a Full Lotus Layback they separated with only five hundred feet remaining to open their chutes.

The audience had gone crazy. The needle on the aerial seismograph pegged way past ten, bounced back to zero, and finally settled down right on top of nine point nine.

"Holy bands of fat succulent sheep," Coyote yelled at Ava, "look at that reading."

Ava took Coyote's hand. "Ahhhh . . . it was nothing," she said, as she leaned against him. "What they did was technically perfect, but it didn't have any real soul to it. There was no joy or laughter. Why, we'll blow that needle so far past the theories of advanced mathematics it will take these whiz kids twenty-five years just to discover the formula of our first move." She punched his arm. "Right?"

Coyote put his arm around Ava. "Sure," he answered, as he thought about the changes he wanted to make in their routine. A round, bald man walked past the platform, bowed and sat down underneath a juniper tree. Coyote waved, and started to say something when the loud speakers crackled and the announcer's voice came over the stadium.

"Ladies and Gentlemen, may I have your attention." The shuffling of papers could be heard. "The balloon judges have given team number five a score of nine point nine-five; the ground judges awarded them a nine point nine for their landing. With their one point bonus for leaving the aircraft at five thousand feet and the nine point nine-five on the seismograph, their total score is . . . nine point nine three!"

The people in the stadium were clapping, shouting and yelling. They had never seen such an incredible execution of The Satori Trilogy performed so expertly and they couldn't wait until the next performance.

Coyote looked back to where Molly's Gandhi Dancer was hanging over the Fifth Mesa. "Keep it shining, you guys, you're getting me stoked," he said under his breath.

"What are you talking about?" Ava asked.

"Nothing . . . nothing at all." He took her hand as they walked

165

over to the ground judge. "I would like to change our routine," Coyote said casually.

Ava stopped. "What?"

Coyote grinned. "Sure, why not?"

Ava's face was outlined in a bank of lights with her curly blond hair tightly suspended around her wide-cheeked face. "You're crazy."

The judge walked over to them. "You'll be going up in that Sopwith over there." She pointed to the biplane.

Ava kicked Coyote on the shins. "We don't have time."

He kissed her. "It's okay." He raised one finger. "I'll be right back."

"What are you talking about?" Ava demanded.

"Well," he answered, "I just thought we could put in a little Mesa Five wizardry."

Ava whacked her head with the heel of her hand. "Coyote, you haven't done any of your Fifth Mesa tricks since you left." She grabbed his arm. "And that was over ten years ago."

He laughed, and looked over at the announcer. "I know." He broke away. "But I can feel it . . . I really can."

"Damn it Tues," Ava shouted, "we're going to stick with our routine." She took his arm. "Anything else would be suicide."

"With the Coyote?"

"Especially with the Coyote."

He raised his hand. "Okay, okay . . . just let me make this announcement."

"Okay . . . but don't do anything weird."

Backing away, Coyote nodded to Ava as he hobbled up the platform's stairs. He asked the announcer if he could use the microphone. He slowly turned in a circle. "Ladies and gentlemen," he began, "I would like to thank Molly Rose and my brother, Kid Monday, for producing this festival. They couldn't make it, but in their behalf I would like to thank all of you for being here. It's a great honor for us, and I hope that we can continue to have these festivals at Wandering Foot instead of what went on here for such a long time. Also, I would like to tell you that my partner, Ava Matisse, and I have decided to change our routine from Seven Moons Seven to ah . . . Coyote Silk." He looked over at Ava and winked. "Thank you, and may we all find peace and happiness on the Third Mesa."

There was a termendous applause as Ava and Coyote walked

over to the Sopwith. A flight attendant placed a ladder behind the starboard wing. Coyote gave him the thumbs-up. A jazz band came marching onto the field. "Damn it Coyote, I told you we can't make any changes."

"Come on, Ava . . ."

"No way!" she shouted. She climbed up the ladder and out onto her wing seat. The pilot motioned to the ground crew to prop the engine. She lowered her goggles and checked her chutes. Coyote signaled to the pilot that he was also ready. Two crew members jerked the wheel chocks as the pilot revved up the engine. He looked over at Ava and then Coyote. Two thumbs-up. The bi-plane started roaring down the runway.

One hundred, one-fifty, two hundred, and then the pilot pulled back on the stick and they were airborn. The airplane banked to starboard and started to climb. The high altitude flood lights traced their movement.

At the prearranged altitude of fifteen thousand feet, the pilot banked one hundred and eighty degrees and headed back toward the drop zone. Just before they reached the stadium he flashed the signal and the two skydivers unsnapped their seat straps. One hundred feet past the drop zone the Sopwith flipped over and Coyote and Ava dropped into space.

Cut away, and someplace where Coyote felt like he had some breathing room, he knew that something big would happen. That old tingling sensation was back, and he was beginning to feel prime. It took them three seconds to stablize, and when they reached terminal velocity, they stretched their bodies into the frog position. Once in control of their descent, Ava grabbed Coyote's hands as they kicked into double laybacks, and when they came around she slid onto his lap. She waved to the pilot who was circling the hot air balloons.

Once the lights had them centered, Ava started to go through their routine in her head when she realized that her husband looked like a love-sick teenager. "Coyote, what's wrong?"

He smiled, and kissed her nose. "I love you, Ava."

Ava was shocked by Coyote's behavior. "I love you," she replied, nervously, "but I suggest that we begin the routine."

He kissed her again. From the balloon judges' view it looked like Ava and Coyote were completely oblivious to the reality that they were falling at one hundred and seventy-six feet per second.

"Say something poetic or even a little erotic," he said, touching her face.

Ava grabbed Coyote's helmet and looked into his eyes. "Coyote, are you on drugs or something?"

Coyote grinned. "No, I'm just happy."

Ava glanced at her wrist computer. "We've lost two thousand feet."

"Ahhh . . . what's a few feet among lovers?"

"Damn it!" Ava shouted, "I'm frightened."

"Let's make love," he said.

"What?" She looked down. "I'm getting out of here." She tried to break away but he held her wrists.

"I'm serious, Ava . . . let's make love."

Ava stopped fighting and looked once again into his eyes. "My God, Coyote, you are serious."

The judges were frantically yelling to each other, calling to the ground crew, and urging Ava and Coyote to open their chutes. "It looks like Tuesday Coyote has frozen," one of them said to the head ground judge.

"I think I can make love now."

Ava looked around at the aerial judges. "Here?"

"Yes, right here." He kissed her hands. "Remember back at the Aerie when you mentioned that we had never made love in the air."

"Coyote, I was . . ."

"I know, but I'm serious."

Ava closed her eyes and leaned against him. "You think you can?"

"I know I can."

Ava opened her eyes and studied his face. "You're mad . . ."

"I know . . . but we won't be hurt, I promise." He kissed her lips. "My magic's back," he said softly.

Once again, Ava looked at the ground and then back at her husband. His eyes were so gentle, and all of his anger had somehow disappeared. She touched his face. She smiled, slowly nodding her head. Why not, she thought to herself, the Third Mesa could stand a little love making right now. She laughed. Or, even a lot. "I love you . . . dearest Coyote." She reached over and unbuckled his harness. "Chutes and everything . . . ?"

Coyote took off her helmet and chutes and let them drop. "I

never did like making love with clothes on," he said, as he removed his chutes. "This is the way it really is anyway, isn't it? Spinning through space without any safety net. And eventually, someone has to take hold of another person and keep the faith."

"No contracts or guarantees," Molly answered, as she threw his helmet away.

Slowly, like twins floating inside a womb, they began to make love—oblivious to everything—consummating the end of Coyote's eternal war.

Falling in supreme ecstasy
like the first couple on the Third Mesa
flying through the godsong with all of the Holy People
The Great Mother laughing within the depth of her vast beauty
Spider Woman weaving another Mesa
The Whoa Man flooding their bodies with his new formula of Double to the Ninth Kalvalya Orgasm (supercedes Mesa 5 Mental Orgasm[9] M Trine)
The Gandhi Dancer, like a fertilized ovum balancing the axis of their orbit
Mona with pom-poms cheering along the outer edges
Kid Monday breathing like a bassoon in the double forte of his love for his brother
Pollen Boy dancing within the bodies sprinkling the golden dust
and soon a light, like an embryonic sac, formed around them which caused their speed to be diminished in half
a nimbus
that continued to grow larger and brighter until they were rocking ever so slowly to
earth
the guests, who had been standing in terror, sighed in one breath as they watched the two lovers perform the most courageous act they had ever experienced. It became a smile within them, and then
a deeper breath, and then in admiration they reached out to touch hands
until everyone touched
the beauty of life
humming as one soft voice
yes

When Ava and Coyote were only five hundred feet above the stadium, He opened his eyes and looked into her face. "You are my
moon," he whispered.

"And you, my dearest Coyote, are my moon."

"The light around us is growing larger . . ."

"It has filled the stadium . . ."

"We've done it . . ."

"I know . . ."

"It's our gift . . . "

"The Mesas have their moon back . . ."

"It's the peace moon"

"From the raggedy ol' Coyote . . ."

"And the Matisse paper cut-out . . ."

"Have finally consummated their marriage."

Below, the musicians began to improvise a song that sounded as
if it came out of everyone's heart—interpreting the breath—like a
bird too young to fly—holding it so gently

praying so quietly

to live

without fear or harm

as the first day of peace

rocking slowly back and forth

Ava and Coyote landing as gently as they had made love

stepping out

the sphere remained intact and began to rise

the two performers clasped their hands and bowed

the audience bowed

the moon rose full

Twenty-four drummers began to pound on large cottonwood drums
and the stadium was filled with one heart beat. A moon song blooming at night like the desert datura into full throated white beauties—
pollinated by the thousand voices that could be heard throughout
the Mesas

The moon found its orbit

Coyote and Ava turned in a circle

"It's a perfect moon," she said, as she took Coyote's hand. She
looked into his face where she saw the moon's reflection in his
dark eyes.

Coyote put his arm around her. "What now?"

"I've been thinking about the kids on the Fifth Mesa." They started walking toward the main gate.

"Of course," Coyote answered.

"Bring them back here."

"Great idea . . ."

She put her arm around her husband's waist. "But first, I would like to stop off at that one stand that makes those great blue corn tomales."

"I could eat a dozen."

Ava kissed him on the cheek. "You always were a great lover, Tues."

He smiled as they turned back toward the stadium. "We're great lovers." He kissed her forehead.

At the food booth they bought a dozen tomales and two large bottles of dark beer. Ava made up a small pack and they headed for the river. A cool spring breeze was blowing from Double Lightning Falls, and the cattails were almost as high as their heads. A Great Blue heron, fishing by moonlight, took flight as two fish jumped upriver.

They walked in silence. Soon they lost the lights from the festival and everything became hushed—muted and sweet—with only the moon to guide them through the canyon. They were happy to be on foot and away from the festivities. It felt so easy. Coyote had lost his limp and every so often he would chuckle, shake his head, and then laugh. Ava walked as if she were holding a child's tear in her palm with the moon's reflection centered inside. A small gift of peace within the clapping hand of Wandering Foot.

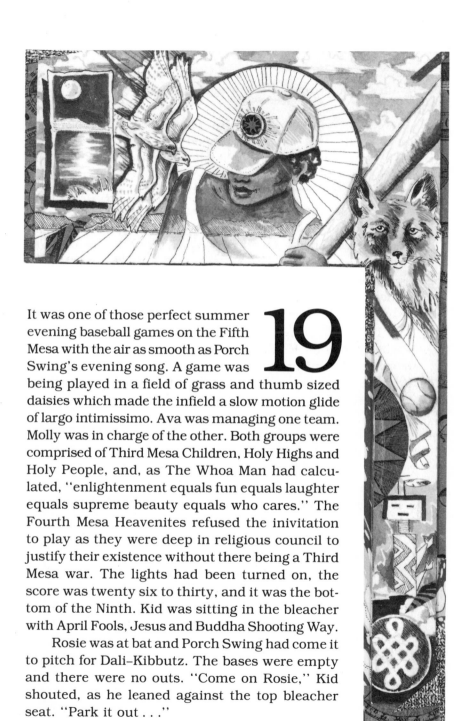

It was one of those perfect summer evening baseball games on the Fifth Mesa with the air as smooth as Porch Swing's evening song. A game was being played in a field of grass and thumb sized daisies which made the infield a slow motion glide of largo intimissimo. Ava was managing one team. Molly was in charge of the other. Both groups were comprised of Third Mesa Children, Holy Highs and Holy People, and, as The Whoa Man had calculated, "enlightenment equals fun equals laughter equals supreme beauty equals who cares." The Fourth Mesa Heavenites refused the inivitation to play as they were deep in religious council to justify their existence without there being a Third Mesa war. The lights had been turned on, the score was twenty six to thirty, and it was the bottom of the Ninth. Kid was sitting in the bleacher with April Fools, Jesus and Buddha Shooting Way.

Rosie was at bat and Porch Swing had come it to pitch for Dali–Kibbutz. The bases were empty and there were no outs. "Come on Rosie," Kid shouted, as he leaned against the top bleacher seat. "Park it out . . ."

"How come Curve Ball isn't pitching?" Jesus asked Buddha Shooting Way.

Buddha Shooting Way had just stuffed a hot dog into his mouth. "He pointed and shrugged. "Mrgrughx szff wrtffythmnmc aoargpffnn."

"Oh yeah, now I understand why you reached supreme enlightenment through silence," Jesus replied.

"Make it mysterious and they'll follow you everywhere," April Fools added.

"You'd better watch out, J.C.," Kid said, as he leaned forward. "Shooting Way is preparing to ride a double lightning bolt through a forty-one day fast while only wearing designer smiles."

Shooting Way threw a wad of paper at Kid. "Blessed are the motor mouths."

"Come on Rosie babe . . . it only takes one."

Ava was giving hand signals to Porch Swing. "Hunker down, P.S.," she said, "hunker down . . ."

"Hey Kid," Coyote shouted from underneath the bleachers. "Look what I've got." He lifted up a large brown paper bag.

Kid leaned down through the seats. "What's up?"

"You are." He lifted a quart jar from the bag. "Treats."

"What's in there?"

"Never mind, just get down here." He wagged his head and started walking past first base. Kid swung down and ran after his brother. Coyote had on a pair of cut-offs, a Mesa Five baseball cap and an old pair of Red Ball Jets he had found in Spider Woman's trunk. His hair was short and he had only the slightest hint of a limp. He waved to his mother who was selecting a bat.

Kid caught up with Coyote. "Oh shit," he said, when he saw Coyote unscrew one of the lids and take a long drink. "Home brew?"

A smile flashed through his dark eyes that ended up in a cock-eyed grin. "A little yeasty yet, but not too bad considering the ingredients." He held the jar underneath Kid's nose. "Ahhh . . . the bouquet of old socks, navel lint and Fourth Mesa gun powder."

Kid lifted the jar from his brother's hand. "Where did you brew this?"

"Ahhhh . . . in the golden bell of Cheyenne Rose." He laughed and motioned for Kid to drink up.

"Ugh . . . ," Kid groaned, as he shook his head. "This wasn't made in my old trombone, " he said, as he cleared his throat. "More

174

like Nuclear Spud's waste dump."

"There's just about enough for our trip back to the Third Mesa," Coyote said as he took back the jar. "Providing that I'm able to slip a quart into each of the little darling's packs." He took a long swallow and smacked his lips. "Good stuff."

Rosie hit a slow roller through the infield. "Atta girl," Kid shouted. Molly stepped out of the dugout and noticed her husband with Coyote. Kid waved, blew her a kiss and pointed toward the rim that looked out over Wandering Foot. She nodded, and waved them off.

Coyote spun the lid back on the jar and put it into the wrinkled sack. He put his arm around Kid's shoulders as they began to walk slowly through the grass. He pointed out to right field. "That's a good place for The Cowboy Buddha," he said, as he waved to the Holy Highs' agent and biographer. "Where there's enough space to tap dance and tai chi at the same time."

It was an hour after dusk and the air was beginning to lose its afternoon heat. Coyote rubbed his chest and slapped his flat stomach. "Are you packed?"

Kid nodded. "Yeah, I suppose, but it's kinda hard to figure out how much to take."

"Take Cheyenne Rose," Coyote said, as he thumped Kid's head. "The bottomless Christmas present." He laughed and found a twig to stick in his mouth.

Kid looked back at the diamond. Doctor King was knocking the mud off his cleats. "So, what do you think about Mona going down to the Fourth Mesa?"

"A little female among all that Scrotum und Yang just might balance that mesa out," Coyote replied. "After what she's gone through she'll be able to push those boys around." He laughed and flexed his muscles. "Mona ain't gonna take no shit from nobody . . . especially The Old Testament."

"And she'll sit on Mohammed's face if his Koran gets too far out of whack," Kid added. He clenched his fists. "Good ol' Mom. All of that power lifting has to be good for something." He punched his brother's arm. "Maybe she'll marry Darwin."

"Marriage is hot right now, brother."

"You're telling me?" Kid looked around the mesa. "Everything seems to be running a lot smoother since Spider Woman took over the Fifth," Kid said, as he stuck his hands into the pockets of his faded jeans. He had on a tank top and his wizard's cap. His eyes had taken on the color of the grass, and his nose was covered with freckles. They came to the edge of the mesa. A new moon was rising over Wandering Foot. "You guys did good," Kid added, as he pointed at the moon.

"It's amazin' what a little Mesa Five love makin' can do," Coyote said in a cowboy drawl. He opened the bag and handed Kid one of the jars. "Because you're such a light weight, Kid Monday, I'll have the full one." Lao-tsu stepped into the batter's box.

"Come on Loud Sue," Kid yelled, as he unscrewed the lid. He clinked Coyote's jar. "Here's to the Coyote Fat's Brewery," Kid said.

Coyote shook his head. "The Coyote Fats and Buddy Sunday Brewery . . . distillers of fine young wizards in their secret Big Mona Malt."

"All right . . . here's to moms and dads and dads and moms . . . and Loud Sue. Park it out . . . ," he yelled.

"Wherever they might be flying in the peace wheel of selected Jui Jui of Jesus." They gave each other High Fives and Low Fives, Behind the Back Fives and Under The Leg Fives. Two Gyre falcons came screaming past in vertical dives. Coyote leaned over the edge and followed their descent. "It must be love."

Kid knelt down and tied his shoe. Lao-tsu hit into a double play. "Spider Woman and Leonardo are coming down as soon as we get settled."

Coyote turned slowly around in a circle. "I'm going to miss this place."

"Whoa," Kid replied, "what's this I'm hearing?" He stood up.

Coyote took another drink and wiped the foam from his mouth. "I never thought I'd hear myself say that." He looked back at the diamond to see who was at bat. "Come on . . . Jamal."

Kid took a sip, winced, and then emptied the jar. "Ohhh . . . this stuff tastes like diesel fuel and smells like cougar come."

"I was trying to teach Thermos how to make good home brew but he just wasn't interested."

"They don't need it," Kid answered.

"Running amok in eternal bliss."

Kid raised his jar. "Sweet dumb fucks."

Coyote laughed because he had never heard his brother use that word. "Hey . . . the famous wizard is learnin' how to cuss a little."

"Hey brother," Kid answered, "we might be Holy Foss but deep down inside where the wolves howl all night and the ghost seeds ride the gospel hump all day long, we're just a couple of slobs from the wrong side of our mother's ovaries." He winked and patted his chest.

Coyote clenched his fists and pumped his arms. "Holy, Holy, Holy . . ."

Kid, captured by the mood of feeling so good with his brother, slapped his pockets and fished out an old package of cigarettes. He tossed them to Coyote. "I found these the other day."

Coyote examined the wrinkled package. "This is the pack I copped from the guards at the Onsen." He opened the package and stuck his nose inside. "Ah yes . . . when you were off serenading Wandering Foot with your piccolo." He took another whiff. "Ahhh . . . how sweet." He ripped open the package and handed one of the two remaining cigarettes to Kid. "Remind me to start growing tobacco when we get settled."

"Sure . . ."

"Hey, I'm serious." Instinctively, he slapped his pockets for a match. "Tobacco . . . , fine grains for double distilled potions and grapes for the Cowboy Buddha's winery of dueling consciousness." He ran the cigarette under his nose. "Naw . . . Holy People don't need that shit . . . right?"

Kid found a match in his tweed coat and struck it on the zipper of his jeans. "I just had a flash that we should hide behind that oak tree."

"Like when we were kids."

Jamal, who had taken a full count, smacked a line drive between first and second. Coyote jumped into the air and shook his fist. "Atta boy, Jamal."

"This cigarette is making me dizzy."

Coyote took a drag and looked at the cigarette as if he were trying to understand what he was smoking. "These two butts are probably the last two in the whole goddamn mesas."

"You'll always find something to smoke," Kid replied. "It's just the weirdness of you."

Coyote laughed. "I always do . . ."

"Look who's coming to bat," Kid said, and the bases are loaded."

Coyote leaned around the tree. "Hey . . . Monaaaaahhhh."

"Ava's making a pitching change."

"Wow . . . she's bringing in The Whoa Man . . ."

177

"What a duel," Kid added.

"She'll kill him."

"Bullshit . . . Coyote, he's got a fastball that starts somewhere inside the suction of a collapsing giant nova."

"With all that pumping iron shit. No way . . . ," Coyote challenged. "It's a cake walk . . ."

"He'll smoke her like he smoked you and Ava back to Paris."

"Hundred bucks says she'll take it all the way downtown."

"You're on . . ."

They looked at each other and then started laughing. "Who's got a hundred bucks, anyway."

"We'll print some when we get back to Wandering Foot," Coyote suggested.

"Maybe Gutenberg stayed on after the festival," Kid replied. "If not, we'll get Leonardo to draw some for us. He can do anything."

"Get him going on the wine making . . ."

Kid wrapped his arm around his brother's neck. "You are a rotten fucker . . ."

"Look . . . The Whoa Man's winding up," Coyote shouted, as he tried to throw Kid onto the grass.

"Ah ha . . . strike one," Kid challenged. He started knuckling Coyote's hair. "I'll bet you've already got some opium poppies growing around here somewhere."

"Park it . . . Mona."

"Haven't you?"

"No way . . ."

"She's the oldest broad in the universe, Whoa Man . . . pay her no mind."

"Hey," Coyote shouted, as he broke loose and pushed Kid away, "don't talk about my mother like that." He clenched his fists and made like he was boxing. "Put up your dukes."

"Strike two," Kid yelled. He started rubbing his hands together. "A hundred bucks will buy us a subscription to the Farmer's Almanac. You're going to need it."

"Hey Mona . . . knock it past the godsong."

The Whoa Man went into his famous triple wind-up that was calculated to send the ball along an electromagnetic current at twenty thousand miles an hour.

Mona pounded on the plate

Ava tried to calm her pitcher down with good trade route vibes

Molly clenched her fists and spoke atta-girl under her breath

time stopped

hotdogs stopped sizzling

hummingbirds hovered in silent mode

the guests who had stayed on at Wandering Foot stopped working on the main villa

Cheyenne Rose glowed

The Cowboy Buddha headed toward the Ninth Mesa

Jesus started tap dancing on the duck pond next to the baseball diamond

Leonardo was painting Mona's picture

Pollen Boy hunkered down behind the plate

Mona's muscles quivered as she stood up in short-shorts, a lavender tank top, white aerobic shoes with tassled socks

The Whoa Man whirled

Mona stared

Put it there . . . brother

Watch this . . . sister

Give me your best shot . . . boy

Your barefoot and pregnant . . . whoaman

I've got your balls . . . baby

One Hand clapped

The Sozu at Wandering Foot paused

Kid and Coyote wrapped their arms around each other's shoulders

Speechless

There was one second where all of the mesas were actually one reality

The Whoa Man's right arm looked like a hyperactive Tibetan Knot of Eternity

Mona wasn't fooled with the mystical tomfoolery

The Whoa Man's brains started to smoke

More deceptions

Mona saw Darwin and Henri Matisse riding a giant turtle back to Wandering Foot.

He delivered

A high ribbon of fire that popped and crackled

She leaned back and smiled, religiosamente

And swung

The Whoa Man disappeared into a cloud of smoke

There was an enormous crack

Leonardo caught the smile

Everyone froze

As they watched the ball sail

away and away with all of the Holy Highs embossed on the horsehide

it looked like The Gandhi Dancer sailing away to the Ninth Mesa

"All right, all right," Coyote shouted, as he jumped up and down. "Atta girl . . . Mona."

Kid dropped to his knees, bowed his head, and then rolled backwards into the grass and flowers. "It's long gone to number nine . . ."

Mona was slowly rounding the bases

Coyote grinned and dropped down beside Kid. "Did you see where that ball went . . . brother Monday?"

Kid leaned on his left elbow. "I lost it somewhere past The Great Medicine Trail . . . hoss." He laughed, and dropped back into floating with the clouds. "The score is finally tied, brother Tuesday, and we can finally go home."

"That's right," Coyote replied, "and now, my older and definitely uglier lookin' twin, you owe me one hundred simoleans." He slapped Kid's knee and laid his head on his brother's stomach.

"Look at that," Kid said to Coyote, "already Holy Man and Holy Woman are inside Mona's ball making love . . ."

Coyote cupped his hand over his eyes and pretended to look past the Seventh Mesa. "And Jesus is preaching The Sermon on the Mount." He flopped back, slapped Kid's leg and threw a handful of grass into his face. "Y'know . . . ," he said, as he placed the empty jar on his belly, "it seems to be one of the special nights, wouldn't you say?"

Kid smiled and let the words drift down through his thoughts as he rode his feelings inside the sweetness of the grass, the sounds coming from the game and the smell of the early evening air. He started to think about when they were in Mona's womb with all of the skydiving, partying, and trouble making they did. And Coyote, naturally, had grown opium poppies somewhere behind her fallopian tubes. It was great back then. He lifted up his head and messed up Coyote's hair. "We've passed Coyote Ugly, hoss, and we've superseded Coyote Fats, so . . . like you say, Tues, it must be one of those Coyote Silk nights."

Coyote laughed and stuck a grass stem into his mouth. He

thought he could see The Great Mother's ball floating way beyond the Ninth Mesa. He shrugged, and looked over at the diamond. Mona was carrying The Whoa Man around the bases on her shoulders, the kids were running all over the stands and the game had been called off until whenever. It didn't seem to make any difference when it would resume. Ava and Molly were walking arm in arm with Spider Woman, and they were ankle deep in wild flowers and grasses. Tomorrow, Coyote thought, they would head back to Wandering Foot, and he was beginning to feel just like a kid once again. The future was all there, and every second was a miracle. He reached over and took his brother's hand. "Yo . . . ," he said, as he squeezed Kid's long slender fingers, "it's just one of those good nights once again."